Boys in the Street

Edward Halpern

ACKNOWLEDGEMENTS

Thank you Phyllis. I couldn't do this without you.
Thank you Jennifer for your help.

Chapter 1

Janet winked at March as he turned back to look at her. She was doing a high kick step. Behind him the two other girls in the trio were following her lead as she energetically did the routine, moving faster and much more gracefully than the other two. The audience was part of the energy now; clapping, swaying and mouthing noises to the music. March gracefully left the small stage, his thirty minute comedy stunt over for this show. The next show would go on in two hours, at ten P.M.

The club was not that small, about three hundred people were jammed in, sitting around small round tables, thick smoke looking like a Fourth of July barbecue in Los Angeles. The noise was throbbing so much it was difficult listening to someone sitting at the same table as you.

March leaned against the curtain in the wing of stage right. His tux catching all the sweat of his night's work, his body draining energy. It was hard work, even for a twenty three year old body in good shape, and two more shows to go before the nights was over. March looked at Janet dancing to the vamping sounds of the trio. *Boy they're good.* He thought to himself. *So was Janet.* He studied her. In her spike heels she was taller than March, he wondered how she could dance in those things. He studied her long legs, very slim, very shapely. *She doesn't have an ass.* He said to himself. *Just legs from the floor to her waist.* She has a thin, lean body with muscles and definitions in the right places. Her breasts were small but upright without a bra, which she never wore, revealing large nipples pushing against her dancing outfit. March watched as her long arms moved around her body and her body moved around the stage, her short curly hair bright in the spotlights twinkling with honey gold and red tones; all natural.

She's beautiful... March said, almost out loud, to himself *...too bad she's such a slut.*

Janet slithered off the stage as the music to her number ended. She walked over to March and dropped her long arms on his shoulders and her right knee between his legs. "Like my work?" she asked.

He smiled at her and nodded.

"It's your birthday, she said. "Ready for your present?"

"Not my birthday yet." March answered "But

I'll take my present now."

"Are you over twenty-one?" she asked.

"Sure." he said.

"Good, because you have to be over twenty-one or I can't do it."

"Oh, I guess I'm in for something wicked?" he said.

"Wicked and wet."

"Sounds great."

"Tastes great too!" she said.

March took her elbow and led her toward the dressing rooms.

"No no." She said, shaking her head. "Too much traffic."

"Where should we go?"

"Bathroom, we'll lock the door."

"Okay with me." he said.

They locked the door, it was very small in the bathroom.

"Take off your clothes." she ordered. "It's your birthday, you should be in your birthday suit!"

They both stripped.

"Ok." she said, "My treat, pick a hole."

Chapter 2

Gill Grayson sat back in the chair. His wrinkled hands were wrapped around a cup of smoking black coffee and a cigarette dancing in his mouth as he spoke. The gray white puffs plumed into the face of March as Gill continued to probe him, asking questions and writing down the answers as he wanted them answered.

"Cold winter, isn't it March?"

"It'll get colder. Westport really freezes over, but I like it this way. I guess I'm used to it by now!" March pulled the collar of his sweater tightly around his neck.

"You're not sorry you moved to Connecticut, are you? You sound lost. In a way you must miss the action!"

"In a way I do." March mused. "But I also like my life now. The quiet isn't hard for me to take. I guess the hectic years arc gone, though I still do club work now and then, but mostly television."

"March, how did it start? You didn't have an

agent. How did you break into the business?"

March studied Gill Grayson. He'd known Gill since his early twenties, almost 60 years ago. Gill hadn't changed much in all those years. Still the mild mannered reporter for the Daily Mirror, still covering the entertainment desk. A friendship between them had developed over the years. Gill did March's first interview; then a young rising comic.

March's memory drifted back to his childhood as he told Gill Grayson about his early youth in Brooklyn. The days of hunger and hardship, the fantasies and anxieties of youth and the incredible times on the street of Coney Island and Brighton. His mind drifted to the basement apartment he lived in with his parents and his sister. It was in a six story luxury apartment house, only a few years old and across the street from the beach and the Brighton Beach Baths; a "nice" beach club of the 40s and 50s.

The neighborhood was mixed: middle class and working people mainly consisting of apartments and houses. All 6 floor elevators and buildings. The rent averaged about seventy-five for a one bedroom. The war years of the 1940s were great for the working people of New York City. The Brooklyn Navy Yard was manufacturing and repairing war ships round the clock, most industries were working on a 24 hr. clock.

March's father, Harry, finally got a job as the country was coming out of The Great Depression due to the economic push of the war effort.

March continued his narrative to Gill Grayson. "Finally we had a steady supply of money. Dad was getting a pay check. Of course there were still problems, we couldn't move out of our basement apartment, there weren't any apartments to move into. The Depression had shut the building industry down years ago and all the people coming into New York City, especially Brooklyn to get work, needed someplace to live.

Gill Grayson was looking into the eyes of March Krantz.

"You were day dreaming a few minutes ago, weren't you? I sort of lost you for a while, didn't I?"

"You're still the old fox Gill, reading people's minds."

"So I was right, hum? You spaced out, lost in the void of time, hum?"

"I'm guilty, lost in the void."

"Thinking about what, March?"

"Oh, just the good old days, when I was a young comic in the night spots of New York. You know about 50-60 years ago or so."

"The wine, women and songs, March?"

"Yeah, especially the women. I was thinking back to the fifties, all the broads I met as an entertainer; and all the fun I had with them."

"Dirty old man, hay March?"

"Yeah, I guess so. Look Gill, if you don't have your memories what do you have? I've been married two times, had thousands applaud me, hundreds write about me and I've made millions. Yet I'm still still alone, and in my old age."

"You know a lot of people, and yet you still feel you're alone?"

The tape recorder was still working as they spoke and occasionally Gill would make notes on a yellow pad.

"Notebooks full of people but very few friends. Too bad. I guess most people my age are in the same bowl of soup?"

"Yeah I guess so March." Gill really didn't want to hear about March Krantz's current life. He wanted the interesting stuff. The raw meat so to speak, when March worked for the Boys in the Street, the Brooklyn mobs of the fifties.

"March, let's start in the middle, okay? How did you get into show business?" I asked you before, you didn't have an agent, did you?"

"No I didn't. It started in the Catskill Mountains in the early fifties. I was in my teens and my father helped me get a job in the clothing factory he was working in. He was a "marker" and a pattern maker. I got a job after school and on Saturdays unloading trucks and cleaning up the factory. You know, back breaking collie work for 50 cents an hour."

"What the hell is a marker?"

"He lays out the clothing patterns on a long, wide sheet of paper, sometimes 25 or 30 feet long and traces around the cardboard patterns. The tighter the patterns are placed together the more money is saved because the finished marker paper is placed over a spread about 50 to 150 ply of material, so less fabric is used."

"March I'm so glad you're telling me all this. Okay I'll play, what happens next?"

"The material is cut with an electric up and down knife along the pattern lines and all the bundles are tied and taken to the sewing rooms to be sewn into garments."

"So where do you fit in this scheme?"

"I became friends with Joe "the cutter""

"Joe the Cutter? At last a mob guy!"

"No stupid, Joe the cutter was the cutter in the factory. He cut the layer of fabrics in the bundles to be sewn."

"Oh, I thought you were going to tell me about a mob guy. Oh well!"

"Gill do you want this fucking story or not?" March said in jest.

"Okay, sorry, go ahead."

March relaxed and continued, he knew why Gill was needling him, it was Gill's way.

"Joe worked weekends at the hotels in the Catskills, he was a waiter, and sometimes he worked as a busboy. He did freelance fill in work. The money was great, he made more money on the weekends then he made all week working in the factory and he had fun too. Real fun!"

"With all the girls in the hotels?"

"Yeah, you got it!"

"You lived in Ellenville?"

"Yup, about 90 miles north of New York City, the "Borscht Belt," the Catskill Mountains, "Rip Van Winkle" land."

"Pretty country."

"It's all pretty, Gill, the whole country!"

"The whole planet March, we are lucky to be here."

"Yeah, you're right, when you're right you're ---"

"Yeah I know, so any how…"

"Well Joe and I started working at the resort hotels as a team, we took turns, sometimes we would be the bus boy and sometimes the waiter, and we made good money, which we split. After a few weeks Joe and I quit our jobs at the factory and worked full time at the hotels."

"Real capitalist, hum?"

Hey wise guy, want a drink?"

"I was wondering when you were going to offer."

March got back with the drinks and continued his story.

"Joe had a strong, melodious tenor voice. He was a great singer when he "let go," but he was shy and didn't like to talk in public. He wouldn't sing a note unless he knew the people who were listening personally."

"Shy guy."

"Yeah, he was born in Ellenville on a chicken farm and lived out of town, away from the city crowds (if you could call a town of 5,000 a crowded city). Joe was about twenty years older than me."

"Mid-thirties?"

"Yeah, close to forty. A good looking guy, Polish parents, close family life and he was still single when I met him."

13

"A virgin?"

"Oh god no, plenty of pussy in the hotels. More than anyone needed, and year round too. Well, Joe and I became very good friends fast, as well as working partners. Around me he started loosening up somewhat and as we got to know the guests at the hotels, (Some of them spent all summer) he started humming and then softly singing. Then we started the shtick.

"You're shtick, his singing?"

"Right, he would serve the soup with a loud, brassy "Oh solo me" and I would do a gag. Stuff at the table."

"Like what?"

"I would serve them an empty plate, we had French service at this one hotel, so I would cover the plate with a silver topper and the plate underneath would have nothing on it or one pea; or I would bring them something completely different than they ordered and when they complained I would bring them something different again or an empty plate. Sometimes I would sit down at the table with them and eat or lay on the floor and Joe would drop food in my mouth. Then I got into doing gags at the table, you know dumb joke time.

14

'Do you know where you're your wife was all week while you were running your business in the city? Well don't worry we know where she was ---every night.' It drove husbands crazy, but everyone at the table (except the couple) loved it. Sometimes Joe would break out in song, his rich voice flowing throughout the dining room and I would go behind him and unbuckle his pants as he was singing. Arms extended, his pants would drop to the floor."

"Didn't management stop you?"

"No, they encouraged us, it made the hotel more homely, the guests warmer and friendlier to each other, more open."

"Did some people complain?"

"Oh yes, they sure did."

"How did management handle that?"

"They moved them to a different table, a different station, they were away from the kibitzing on the other side of the room, some of the hotels held 500 guests in the dining rooms. The rooms were large enough to hide our shticks."

One resort hotel we worked at, in Napanoch, a town near Ellenville, was run by Tony Banorluga, a knowledgeable hotel owner who really encouraged me to go on the stage."

"Related to Joe Banorluga, the gangster?"

"His brother, one of five."

"No shit? Wow!"

Gill Grayson was thinking about the Banorluga family. They were involved in the garbage collection business, delivery business, dry cleaning, real estate, ship building, clothing manufacturing, liquor, warehousing and distribution, night clubs, hotels, motels, car rentals, retail stores, restaurants, and on and on.

"Holly shit! How did you get involved with…?"

Gill, I've known you a long time, you knew I worked in clubs owned by the 'Boys', didn't you? We talked before."

"Not like this March, we never talked in detail. I only interviewed for my column or a special piece, not like this. Not in such dctail."

"Yeah, I guess you're right. Okay, so shut up and listen."

Gill nodded and March continued.

"Tony Banorluga took a personal interest in Joe and me. He had a tape recorder set up in the dining room and got tapes of all my stuff. A lot of it was funny, some of the material I'm still doing today, some fifty years later."

Gill shook his head. "You will go on forever March."

"As long as they want me, I'm still here."

"As long as you're funny! Do you still write your own material?"

"About 90 percent. The rest I steal or have scouts who steal material for me, and I pay them by the line, a lot of people in the business do the same."

"Go on."

"Well Tony encouraged Joe and I, he told us we were good enough to work the lounge as an act, together. We could do it and he pushed us. It was hard work. The rehearsals and working tables, it was a day and night thing and almost no time for anything else!"

"You found time for other things, right?"

"Sure, at that age? Girls, what else?"

"Why did you have to rehearse?"

"We didn't really have an act, it was all random shticks, and we needed timing. We had to know how long to stay on stage, the music cues, the spotlighting, what side of the stage to exit; Big Time, you know?"

"They paid for training you?"

"Sure, we were professionals!"

"Yeah, right, amateur night on stage!"

"No, no, no, we were real. We got laughs, applauds, they hollered, they screamed. We related to the people and we were in."

"And Tony Banorluga, he paid you?"

"Yeah, we got per night, to start."

"For each of you?"

"No, not at first, but as the weeks went by and the summer crowds were jumping for joy we got more money. Big bucks, for each of us. The weekend crowds were big because word got around.

Friends came up for the weekends, etc."

"Just to see you guys? The teenage amateur and the almost forty singer? You were that good?"

"Sure Gill, look at Vegas, the big names draw crowds. People coming up to the Catskills had a decision to make: which hotel."

"You drew them in, and in only one summer? They drove the ninety miles to see you both? That's what you're telling me?"

"Tony told us attendance was up over 20 percent over any other summer and the bar and lounge were packed for all the shows. Tony started taking reservations and the people lined up. Even the townspeople were coming."

"Wow."

The best part of this was the publicity, a small town boy makes good."

Good news, good times, hey March?"

"I was young and having a ball."

"Yeah, and getting paid too, what a racket!"

"Tony did well so we did well."

"What do you mean? What's 'well.'"

"Good money, don't forget it was the early 50's. People were making fifty dollars a week!"

"So tell me, how much were you making?"

"To start fifty a night each, toward the end of the summer we were getting more."

"How much is more?"

"None of your fucking business, Gill!"

"Okay guy, does this end the interview?"

March was quiet for a long minute, then he locked his fingers together before answering Gill Grayson.

"Just the reaction of an old man, sorry Gill."

"Old man with a short temper, hey March?"

"Yeah I guess that's me. One hundred sixty pounds of dynamite with a short fuse."

"Short everything, hey March?"

"Yeah, okay." March laughed and rolled his eyes. "That's me. I guess I lived alone too long."

"Ready?" Gill asked.

20

"Yeah, I'll go on, sorry for the outburst."

Grayson knew how to handle people.

"There I was… A snot nosed kid with big money in his jeans."

Gill nodded at March.

"Twenty five dollars a performance made seventy five dollars a night. They paid me cash out of the bar register."

"You were still a waiter?"

"Oh yeah. Still working my station. Ten people to a table, four to five tables. Lots of hard work for ninety dollars a month plus room and board; not including tips. Life was good. Very good."

"What did you do with all the money?"

"Bought a car."

"New car?"

"No used. Pontiac Chieftain with a straight eight cylinder. Paid in cash."

"Oh you were hot stuff with everyone."

"I thought so. Big dick car. The back seat was a

bedroom, everything but a king size bed. Sometimes I had two girls at once. If we would go to a motel, a crowd of us, I would pay everything. Dinner, rooms, everything. I didn't know what money could do and I couldn't spend it fast enough!"

"New clothes, March?"

"Oh yeah I bought new clothes. Real clothes, in department stores. We found time to go to Kingston, the big city, and Joe and I went shopping at Sears or Penny's or something like that. I don't remember which one, but we went shopping big time. It was all in cash. That's all people had, very few people used checks and credit cards back then, cash mainly. I had several hundred in my roll and so did Joe. Big money back then. We went straight to the men's department where this blonde floozy helped us pick out some real sharp suits we could use on stage. Then she told us her life story. We told her we were entertainers. It was somewhat true, why tell her we were waiters? Well she went nuts over us. We could have had her in the fitting room!"

"Both of you? At once?"

"Yep." March rubbed his hands together and then rubbed his knees, excited at the memory.

"Yeah, go on."

"When we pulled out the wads of money to pay she became glued. Hung on Joe's arm and wouldn't let go of him."

"So?"

"So, being gentlemen, we took her to a motel for a body adjustment."

"The three of you?"

Yeah Gill, just the three of us. We had to call the hotel and tell Tony we would be late. The Pontiac broke down, what a way to go."

"She didn't want to invite a girlfriend?"

"No, no time, we didn't go out for dinner, she wasn't interested in food. Just the entertainers.

"So you guys got the taste of power."

"Exactly Gill, that's what started it."

"And the money closed the deal."

"Right. From then on, I knew I was something special."

"Were you?"

I thought so then, but the years proved me wrong. Somehow I became lost, and lonely."

"The trademark of many public people. Lost in their private lives."

"I guess so. Too much too fast."

"You need the hard times to balance the good times."

"I guess so." March was becoming uncomfortable with the conversation now. His mixed-up personal life was not one of his favorite topics. Many of the professionals loved their careers but couldn't control their own habits. Their desires, their demons... March resifted his weight in the arm chair, then he stood up and walked around the room.

Gill knew he was uncomfortable talking about his private family life and his big failure. Not to mention his two wives and now his loneliness. He waited for March to direct the conversation, letting him pick the subjects. Gill didn't want to end this interview, it was good "Copy." March was a well-known celebrity, and even at his late age still made headlines. Gill felt the interview would last several days and fill many hours of reading time. Maybe even a book for Gill, his seventeenth. Gill patiently waited for March to continue.

"Want dinner?" March asked.

"Not now, it's too early."

"I have to order in, it takes time. I'm between housekeepers now."

"You used to have a young lady who helped you keep house, what happened to her?"

"Pretty young thing Debbie? She jumped in bed with me and then started to tell me how to live and how to spend my money."

"So you're alone again?"

"Someone, somewhere will pop-up, they always do. Sometimes they will work here for nothing, just to be with me."

"Name recognition?"

"Yeah, groupies, they love to hang on. That was Debby; and many others."

March continued his small talk until dinner was delivered. A gourmet dinner from a local fine restaurant, complete with tableware and linen.

March didn't care about cost, he was beyond watching his money, and at his advanced age he knew he would never spend it all. No one to leave it to meant no worries. They ate and drank at a slow pace, both having no place to go and enjoying each other's company. After dinner they both smoked cigars, a Montecristo, and continued late into the evening.

March told Gill Grayson about the other resort hotels he had worked at as a young man, hunting for his place in the world. He told Gill about the time a singing trio, three sisters, were engaged to work at one of the hotels he was working in. March had finished cleaning up his station and it was almost nine at night. The dining room manager had asked him to stay on to serve a late supper to the trio and their entourage. The manager told March to wait in the dining room for them as they would soon be in to eat. March waited till almost eleven before they sat down. The dining area in this hotel was enormous, it could and often did seat twelve hundred guests in one seating. That meant almost two hundred feet from the kitchen to March's station. Back and forth, back and forth. Walk your body into submission before the day is over. They swaggered into the dining room wearing wet clothing. It was raining. They were arguing, yelling at each other and rude to March.

"Where are you, boy?!"

He was standing at the table, in plain sight of everyone.

"The soups not hot enough, bring us hot food! Hurry, come on we're tired!" The whining didn't stop.

Fucking pigs. Thought March. *I'll give you hot soup alright.* He went into the kitchen and turned up the cooking gas under the pot of soup. March was tired and pissed. He carried a large bowl of hot soup to the table and then slowly and methodically spilled it on each of the five people in the group. Then he ran out of the dining room, went to the dormitory, got his personal stuff and rushed out of the hotel. He knew if the security goons would catch him, they would beat the hell out of him; maybe bury him in the mud and rain. There was a lot of construction around the hotel area, easy to bury someone in cement. He slept on a board with a thin mattress, pillow and light weight blanket. The beds were stacked three high and the dorm could sleep seventy-five people. It was as if you were in a German concentration camp.

"My car was stuck in the mud. The employee

parking lot was not paved and there was a wet pool of mud. There was a tractor parked nearby, with the key in the ignition. I rushed into the hotel, found someone to drive it and gave him a dollar to pull me free.

"How much did they pay you for your 'military duty'?"

"Military is the right word, Gill, less than twenty percent for room and board, such as it was."

"But wait there's more, Gill. It's been a long life."

"I guess so!"

"One of the resorts I worked for asked some of their help to go to the bar after working hours to act as "sit-ins".

"Explain that March."

"Male prostitutes. We would sit at the cocktail lounges and drink, and the women guests would pick us up. The hotel lounge was noted for its fast crowd. The women were alone all week without company, their husbands came up on the weekends. Most of them owned businesses in New York. It worked out real well for them both- the husbands screwed around all week and the wives picked up the young studs at the hotels."

"Sex was on the march, right March?"

"Good line Gill."

"You really enjoyed yourself!"

"Most of it was good, none of it was great. Some of the women were fat and ugly, or middle aged and nuts, but it was all in a days work and the money was great."

"They gave you money?"

"Sure! Tips, cash, clothes, jewelry, everything."

"The hotels encouraged this?"

"Oh yeah, they gave us tokens to pay for the drinks, which was mostly soda water; but the old chicks really took care of us. Sex was in, except we didn't talk about it the way we do now, we just did it!"

"No AIDS to worry about?"

"There were still bugs, Gill, the doctors were very busy giving us shots."

"Nothing for nothing?"

"We pay for everything, one way or another."

"You said the women were nuts, what did you mean by that?"

"Lonely, unhappy housewives. Too much money and no one to share it with. The husbands worked five, six, seven days a week and late every night and so did their staff. These people were mostly 7th Ave. clothing manufacturers pushing their line. Lots of competition, lots of problems and when they had a good season, lots of money."

"And 'mama' stayed home with the kids?"

"Yeah, that's how it went in those days Gill, most women stayed home with the kids and got fat."

"And bored."

"Yeah fat and bored and the husbands lived a separate life, almost two separate families- especially when the big bucks started coming in after years of struggle."

"Every family March?"

"The ones I knew. In the hotels, they told me

30

their story. Usually we talked with our clothes off."

"Did you work many hotels in the Catskills?"

"No, just a few. That's enough, don't you think?"

March got up again to stretch and pace the room. He was thinking back, more than sixty years ago.

"I worked with my partner, Joe, at a large hotel outside of Ellenville. They had a weekender, a convention, and they needed extra help, so we went. It was a sales meeting and trade show for important buyers. You know, one of those reward weekends for the sales crew? Then at the same time you show new products to the buyers and get orders for future production and the write-off is okay with the tax people."

"Yeah, go on."

"Joe and I worked till nine. All the speeches were over, dinner was over and then we worked the bar. It was an open bar to everyone and at that price, the liquor was fast flowing. The sponsoring company, don't ask me who it was I don't remember, had hired about twenty hookers and bussed them up from New York. At about eleven

31

everything slowed down and Joe and I were paid and told we could go home. So we changed into our suits. We looked like salesmen and fit into the scheme of the evening."

"You joined the party?"

"Yeah man, we picked up two of the call girls and joined the party."

"Where did you take them, you had no rooms?"

We walked over to the empty bus, the door was wide open. Then we were kind enough to let them do their job. Then we switched girls and fell asleep until the bus driver came aboard and chased us off the bus, naked as a jay bird, clothes in hand."

"Not the girls?"

"No, they stayed with the bus, they belonged with the bus."

"Tough life, March." Gill said sarcastically.

"It wasn't always like this."

Chapter 3

The morning haze was giving way to the late spring sun, it was almost summer, and you couldn't tell where the ocean ended and the sky began, but it was all out there waiting for humanity to wake up and enjoy it. Or take it for granted, their choice.

March was up early, the water bugs were crawling all over the small apartment and he didn't sleep well. He put on his corduroys and knitted polo shirt, the one he always wore. He sort of combed his hair, which was too fine and long to stay in place anyway. A glass of water for breakfast (typical for him at seven years of age) and he quietly closed the front door not wanting his parents to wake-up. He often woke up at dawn, the sun's light chased the water bugs back into the walls and signaled the start of his day. It was Friday, a school day for most kids in Brooklyn, except March and his gang of friends. They had arranged it the day before, Friday this week was hooky day, their day off together. They cut class at least once a month so they could "pal out" together as they called it. March walked the block to friend Solly's apartment house. Solly's

33

parents were relatively well off compared to some of the families that lived in Brighton Beach. The depression was still grinding at the life styles of the average family. Food was scarce, clothing worn and tattered and money was owed to every relative that still had some to lend.

Solly's lived in a six floor apartment building, in those days it was considered a good building. Clean, less than twenty years old. Big apartments, an elevator, and Brighton Beach was a good middle class area in the late 30s. The front door had an electric security system. March rattled the door up and down and the lock let go. He walked through the lobby, which was nicer than the basement apartment he lived in, and up the three marble steps to the first floor. He gently knocked on Solly's door. Solly opened it, his finger in front of his nose.

"Shhhh…" He said blowing thru his finger. "They're still sleeping."

Solly carried his school books with him as he left the apartment, quietly shutting the door. They walked arm in arm, laughing as they started to run through the early morning streets. Playing hooky was great fun.

Two blocks away, on the same street was

Stewart, another friend and one of the gang, all pals, buddies since first grade, and one did nothing without the other three, the inner circle. March, Solly, Stewart and Elliot. The four inner core pals of trouble in Brighton, Coney Island and later South Brooklyn. Today's hoods, tomorrow's juvenile delinquents.

The four of them went to Stewart's apartment. After nine in the morning no one was home and they had the place to themselves. They raided the ice box (Stewart's parents hadn't bought a refrigerator, too costly for them). Stewart's dad, Jim, was a salesman for a men's clothing manufacturer in Fall River, Massachusetts and he was on the road several days a week. Bad times for a clothing salesmen. Stewart's mom worked at a grocery store as a clerk and food handler where she helped the butcher cut meat; she did everything, and was glad to have a job.

Stewart, did not like his name shortened to Stew because some wise ass friends started calling him Stew pot and when one wise guy called him toilet instead of pot he had had enough and made sure everyone called him Stewart. Stewart's dad collected adult films during his road travels. He had a big collection on the top shelf of his closet and Stewart knew where they were. So the four of them were watching porno films made in the thirties, all black and white because color wasn't yet in home movies. They watched for two hours and got very bored and all four of them fell asleep.

It was Friday, Jim came home about 1:00 P.M. and found the four boys lazing around. His face was flushed from anger and he got the large stick from the hall closet and started to beat hell out of all of them. March and Elliot jumped out through the window and climbed down the fire escape, Solly ran out the front door leaving Stewart alone with his old man. Stewart took a terrible beating and it wasn't the first time. That's the way you handled kids back then, with a stick or the back of your hand.

Luckily no bones were broken and Jim had a few beers and fell asleep on the couch and Stewart left the apartment even though his father told him he couldn't go out, only for school, for a month.

Stewart caught up with the three boys in Charlie's Candy Store on 6th Street. They were drinking chocolate egg creams, and begging Charlie for free fill-ups when Stewart walked in. March looked at Stewart's face and was shocked. It was swollen and had pink/red welts where blows from the stick had caught him. His cheeks were swollen from Jim's back hand slaps.

"You look like shit." Elliot said.

"Not that bad, he's given me worse before."

"Then you must be dead by now" said March, always throwing out the last word.

"Fuck you."

"Fuck you too, Stew Pot."

They started pushing each other until Charlie broke it up. "Outside, get the hell outside!" he said. "I don't want any broken stuff in here."

The four of them walked out to the street, the candy store was small, with a counter with six stools and a soda fountain behind the counter and loads of candy and cookies in glass jars. Charlie could make you a simple sandwich for twenty or twenty five cents and a fountain soda for five cents. Or you could order a plain soda water for two cents and beg Charlie for some chocolate syrup and maybe he would add it but most of the time he wouldn't do it.

The candy store was small, but the back room was big, and behind the closed door was the card room. The people in Brooklyn loved to play cards, and poker was the big game. Six tables with wire feet and wire chairs, each table could seat eight people shoulder to shoulder and Charlie would charge ten cents out of every pot. Sometimes he would take in forty dollars a day from the poker plus sandwiches, cigarettes, cokes, sodas, and the little extra he made from tips and newspapers. The racing forms and policy slips were a business unto itself. Charlie netted over $300 a week when most people were making $50. He had a near new Buick parked in front of his house which he owned as well as the houses on the left and right of his. All this being said Charlie walked to the candy store or took a bus to work. Nobody who went to the candy store knew Charlie outside of his business life. Grungy, sometimes dirty, with his white apron that always had food stains and his shoes worn out and holey. Charlie looked the part of a small shop keeper, one of hundreds who owned candy stores in the Brooklyn of the late thirties. There was a cop on the beat, Eddie, who knew Charlie ran a card room, but Eddie had a free lunch, smokes, and paper so as long as no one complained, Charlie was free to run the store. And no one would complain. Eddie knew it was a small operation, not hurting anyone. Not to mention Harry's butcher shop down the street had a card table in the back and Mike Lorenzo had 2 tables in his delicatessen. He used to charge twenty cents a pot until the neighborhood players complained to him that other card rooms took ten to twelve cents a pot. So he lowered his take per pot to 12 cents and life went on.

Charlie went outside to see what the four hoodlums were up to. He didn't want to chase them away, he just didn't want any trouble in the store. They were tossing coins against the curb.

"You bums want to make some coins?" he asked. They all got up from their knees and circled around Charlie. Charlie used the boys as runners, a mob term. Charlie had connections to the mob. He was connected to the last ring, the outside circle, but he had the phone numbers of the higher-ups if he needed them. He paid his assessment every month, right on time: fifty dollars. It was his insurance money and it kept him from trouble. No mob guys hanging around his place meant no fights, no broken bones, no broken windows and no prostitutes on his street corner. Eddie the cop was happy and so was Charlie.

The Boys in the Street allowed him to run his policy slip collections. They were not involved in it at all. The collections, sixty percent, went directly to the bookies who worked for the syndicate. The rest of the forty percent Charlie used to run his end of the operation, the money for his runners, ten cents a slip, and pay-outs for the winners, which were few and far between. The scheme worked almost like a lottery. The player would pick up to seven numbers and if all seven won they would receive one-half the money in the big pot collected from all the players. Only the collector would know how much was in the pot, the players were never given the true numbers of dollars to be won. It was all accomplished with greed and hope for the poor people of Brooklyn. The hope was kept alive by the runners, the kids, and ages 7-9 who ran the slips. They picked up the numbers the players picked and the betting money while telling the players how much the winning pot was worth. The policy slips with the numbers, the names, and the amount bet was turned over to Charlie.

Charlie would return some of the cash to his steady players. He would have his top runner, an eighteen year old junkie, Alex, deliver the cash; sometimes as much as $300 if the player picked 5 or 6 numbers correctly. It really happened, and no one ever won the seven number playoff, Charlie made sure of that. Charlie trusted Alex with the payout cash because Alex worked for him for almost ten years and he knew if he crossed Charlie, Charlie had the connections find him and get even.

Charlie gave each boy the day's run, a list of
players to pick up money and policy numbers. A
hand written list of addresses and they were off
running. Each boy would make about twenty-five
pickups and earn $2.50 to $3.00 a day. Four to five
hours of work was easy, especially at their ages.

March knocked on the door of a team captain,
she collected the policy slips in her apartment
building. Today she had thirty five players, not bad,
the six story apartment house had 60 tenants. She
went to each apartment to collect and knew the
approximate hour of each day when the runners
would pick up the slips. It was different each day of
the week so cops wouldn't be waiting for the
runners.

The captain greeted March. "Do you want to
come in for milk and cookies, young man?"

March just stood in the door way and shook his
head. He heard about her from the older boys. They
called her the "Fruit Cake Lady".

She liked to have the boys come in and keep her
company, she was a lonely old woman and since her
husband and all her family had passed away she had
no one to spend time with. It was her habit to keep
people with her as long as possible so she would be

able to talk to them. Sometimes she didn't know how to keep them from leaving so she would take off her clothes and sit there stark naked, the boys half in shock, as she talked. March wanted no part of her. He took her envelope full of money and policy slips, put it in his briefcase, marked her name and address on it, and ran like hell to the next address on the list. The majority of pick-ups were from older people, mostly women, it gave them something to do, besides listening to the radio and clean house. The system was based on hope, Charlie knew that. That's why he paid off. Sometimes the numbers didn't work so he had to make them work by paying so the word would get around and the marks would keep playing.

March climbed up the porch steps and rang the bell. When it didn't work, he pounded on the door of the brownstone. Several moments later and a white bearded man opened the door. They knew each other.

"So, March, why so much noise? I hear you, you know."

"Sorry Mr. Arronwichzh. You took so long to answer the door, I didn't know of you were home."

"I'm always home, unless I'm in schul. You

shouldn't be here, you should be in schul too, yes?"

"I guess so, Mr. Arronwichzh."

"You guess so? How you going to get a bar mitzvah, hum?"

"I'm only seven. Soon it'll be my birthday, I'll be eight."

"Well, you should be in Hebrew school young man, anyway here is your gelt."

March takes the envelope.

"Today I bet a dollar and four quarters. I hope I win, I need it."

So it went, all day long. March made his last pick-up and at four thirty was back in front of Charlie's candy store. Elliot was waiting for him.

"Finish early?" March asked.

"Yeah, had a good run too." he said.

The four boys had grown up in the streets of Brooklyn and their ages were only part of their lives. Experience added years to an already complicated life. Charlie had a saying, "It took a lifetime to live a life."

Stewart and Solly showed up before five thirty. After Charlie paid them they had almost fourteen dollars between them. What to do now?

"Let's go to the movies." said Solly.

"No movies, no movies!" said March. "Friday night, all the guys are in the movies feeling up the girls, I don't want some guy sitting in front of me squeezing his date's tits."

"Then where should we go?" Elliot asked.

"Coney Island!" said Stewart and March together. "Coney Island Coney Island Coney Island!" They were shouting and jumping up and down in a circle.

Charlie came out of the store to see what all the noise was about. He didn't want anything broken.

"Coney Island Coney Island…" they were holding hands and still jumping, they quieted down when Charlie gave them a dirty look, but he was also smiling inside at the youth of the four of them.

"Wish I was going with you." He said.

"You're too old for Coney Island." said Solly.

"Watch your mouth." said Charlie.

They waved him off and headed down the street, toward the trolley tracks. A trolley was going north away from Coney. The four of them hopped the trolley on the back running board and held on for a free ride. They rode about one mile when they spotted another trolley going south, toward Coney Island. They pulled the rope that held the electric connector wheel to the overhead wires and the trolley stopped. The driver came running toward them yelling and waving a bully club. They laughed at him and ran toward the other trolley and hopped aboard the back running board. They were riding for ten minutes when a traffic cop on a horse spotted them. He caught up with them and started hitting on their legs with his night stick. They jumped off the rear bumper and ran in four different directions. The cop didn't follow them; they knew he wouldn't. They met again at the trolley tracks a few blocks away, waited for the next trolley, and hopped back on. After a few blocks away a police car came up behind the trolley and flashed its lights. The boys again ran in four directions. They met after walking a few blocks.

"Let's get some fruit." said March.

"Okay, lets."

45

They walked into a small fruit market on Brighton Beach Boulevard. Two of them stayed together, walking through the market. Touching everything and making lot of noise. The store manager followed them. The other two separated and walked around the store stuffing their pockets with candy bars, bananas, apples and anything else they wanted. Then the two with the stuffed pockets left the store one at a time and after a while the two walking together left, making an Italian gesture at the manager. They got together on the next block, sat down on a parked car to eat and then caught the next trolley for Coney Island. This time they went into the car, paid their five cents each and sat down.

Chapter 4

The Coney Island of the late 1930s and into the mid 40's was the bustling outdoor circus of New York and there was nothing like it any place in the world. Crowded with rides, side shows, games of chance, parlor games and food stands lined the place. The biggest and best was Nathan's Hot Dogs. Hot dogs were five cents, French fries five cents, drinks five cents and free grilled onions, mustard and ketchup. The Hot dogs a foot long made of real meat snapped when you bit into them.

"Oh the good old days, hum!"

Steeple Chase was near Nathan's, all the best stuff was near

Stillwell Avenues. Steeple Chase was the zenith of amusement parks. No violent rides, just fun stuff. It was named after one of its rides, a horse racing ride. You sat on a horse and it raced around the park on steel rails, great fun. The boys ate four hot dogs each with French fries and orange sodas. The sauerkraut was free for the taking and March filled up a plate with sauerkraut and relish piled high on his hot dogs.

When they couldn't eat any more they went into the amusement. It cost less than a dollar to get in and you could get on almost any ride without paying anything more. They stayed in the park until 8:30 and then got lost in the crowds on the streets. They weren't tall enough to see through the crowds but they knew where they were, they had been here many, many times. They stopped at a shooting gallery that cost ten cents. They shot off the load and bought another round and missed every shot again. They walked a few blocks through the night crowd and went into an alley. The alley had side shows and game booth darts, shooting ranges, baseball games, ring toss and lots more to keep four young minds busy.

They went into a side show. The barker did not want them to come in, he said they were "too young". March told him to go screw himself, and they went to another show. They paid 10 cents each to get in. There was a two headed woman, a monkey woman, a snake with a human head, a chicken with two heads, and mouse the size of a large dog. It was a South American capybara, the world's largest rodent. The barker didn't let the boys in so they lifted up the canvas and stood in the back watching. A girl was on stage. The boys watched as she started taking off her clothes and then a man came on the stage with her. He started doing her and then the barker asked if anyone else "wanted it for a dollar?" The boys left, they had seen enough for one day.

They got a cab driver to drive them home. He didn't' want to drive them but they showed him money and said they would buy him a roast beef sandwich at Nathan's, five cents. The cab driver was a world of information, he told the boys about the 75,000 frankfurters sold after 10:00 PM. They couldn't care less. They were almost asleep.

Chapter 5

Light flashes were visible far off on the horizon, the ocean a sea of calm as the sun was taking a daily dip into the sea. The twilight fast becoming night. The boom boom boom far off in the distance but loud enough to cause attention was noticed by the few on the boardwalk. The light flashes looked like lightning in a far away storm, but this was the storm of war. The German submarines were shelling ships before they left for the open seas. The sounds of war were heard in the cities along the coast of America. In New Orleans an axis submarine sunk an American cargo ship at the mouth of the Mississippi, killing twenty-seven people. In June of 1942 eight German saboteurs aboard a submarine were seized by the coast guard as they attempted to land at Amagansett Beach in Long Island, and Ponte Verde Beach in Florida. 1942 was not a good year for America. In October of that year, price control laws were put into effect freezing wages, rents and farm prices. In November 29, 1942 the U.S. began to ration coffee and in December 27 million passenger car owners were told that their gasoline would be rationed to twenty-five to thirty gallons per month. Tires were rationed, meat was rationed, sugar, nylon stockings, it was hard to buy shoes and new cars were not being manufactured. Chrysler was making tanks.

Yet something good happened in December 1942, Christmas, when the movie Bambi opened. A very charming animated story about a young deer and his family and friends. Thumper, a rabbit with a personality that inspires those around and near him.

Flower the skunk who is another true companion to Bambi and a delight to the audience.

Friend owl, the wise reliable chaperon that bestows his wisdom on Bambi. His father, great Prince of all, you have to watch the Disney movie to see all the color, action and warm and emotional feeling of another Disney animated success story. Something America solemnly needed in 1942.

Chapter 6

Summer time was fun time in Brooklyn. The large boilers used to heat the apartment buildings were cleaned out and shut down. The boilers looked like steam locomotives without wheels or cables set up on cylinder blocks in the basement of the building. March Krantz and his group would crawl through the door in front of the boilers and play cards inside, a perfect hideout and private club house.

The smell of ashes lingered and the ash covered their clothes, but who cared? Clean clothes were really unnecessary, that was for grownups. They played poker for pennies and a nickel per pot. March and Solly came up with an idea and they thought it was good. They invited some classmates who lived in the same neighborhood to play poker with them. The only rule was instead of losing money, you take off your clothes. They called the game strip poker. The girls were told about the rules and they said "okay." Besides they had never seen a naked boy and they all thought it was exciting. Three girls, four boys and a deck of marked cards. The gang, I guess you could call them a gang, did crazy mischievous things.

"Nuts. We were nuts then, this was the nut years of my life! We would take the elevator to the sixth floor and walk up the stairs to the roof of the building I lived in.   The beach and the ocean were a half block away separated by the boardwalk. The boardwalk stretched to Coney Island almost two miles away. It was a great view looking out toward the Atlantic Ocean below us, and the beach and all the summer crowds walking to the beach, all six stories below us. All in a holiday mood." The devil was in us, we did horrible things."

"Like what?" asked Gill Grayson.

"We dropped water balloons on people walking on the sidewalk below us. We took cans of water up to the roof and filled balloons and dropped the balloons off the roof."

"Did you drop any on people? Hurt anyone?"

"I don't think so, no. At least we didn't try to drop any on people. Just in front of them, shock them. Now years later, when I think of all the shit I did, sometimes I hate myself."

"You were a juvenile delinquent, weren't you March?"

"Yeah, I guess I was."

"What didn't you do, March?"

"I didn't really hurt anyone, I was more of a smart alleck. Not a mean kid, just wild."

"Oh, the depression was over?"

"Yeah, the war years were all around us. We would collect scrap metal and sell it to junk yards. We stole hub caps off cars and sold them too. Chrome paid a good price during the war."

"Hub caps, you mean wheel covers?"

"Yeah, today they call them wheel covers. Our language is changing."

Gill Grayson looked at March with the penetrating stare that went through you, into your inner thoughts. He shut off the tape recorder and attached a new tape reel.

"Go ahead March." he said.

"Be right back Gill, have to pee."

March returned to the recreation room. It was a warm room, a man's room, some people would call it a family room, but March had no family. No one to call, no one to call him, no family birthday parties, no anniversary cards, no one.

"Have another." March waved the Haig & Haig pinch bottle at Gill.

"Sure, why not?" Gill answered.

"The war changed the way people looked at society. Things were more open, morality changed. Times were moving fast. Women working out of the house. People were interacting with each other, the country became more of a solid mass, one mind, set on winning the war."

"Millions of people dying all over the world. You didn't know if your family member in the service was alive! Horrible times, March."

"I felt the war was justified Gill. That war was justified."

Gill nods in agreement.

March continues. "Too many wars are just political, and they end where they started, with the same results, or worse. People killed, and for what means? Just bad political moves by the world leaders."

"How do you resolve it March?"

55

"I really don't know, I guess no one has the answers at this time. But killing people isn't the answer. The world is too ready to kill. It's too easy because the world society allows it to happen. Just think, the world, in most cases, has little respect for fat people, but allows genocide, mass murder, bombing of non-combatants. The mind set of this planet is sick!"

"Again, how do you resolve it?"

"I don't know. I'm not a world leader, just a critic of the current situation."

"Since you can't resolve it March, let's change the conversation, okay?"

"Yeah you're right, back to the beginning, take one."

"Good, go on."

"The cops were always chasing us as kids…"

Gill smiles and nods for March to continue.

"…The apartment houses were close together. About six or eight feet apart and we would cross on boards from one apartment house to another. We nailed boards together and used the planks as bridges between the buildings."

"Six floors up."

March nodded affirmably.

"Crazy kids, not afraid of anything."

"Yeah that was us, not afraid of anything and willing to do almost anything."

"Did the cops ever come up to the roof?"

"Oh yeah, many times, but we would use the boards to cross from roof to roof, and then take the boards with us."

"The cops didn't catch you guys, they could have come up to both roof tops at once."

"Yeah we knew that. We also knew it would take a lot of time and energy and police power. Besides we weren't that important to them, just a bunch of kids doing nutty things."

"Like dropping water balloons on people, that could have caused some damage to someone; but you didn't think about that, did you?"

"No, not at that age. I told you the devil was in us!

"I guess the devil is in all of us at some time in

57

our lives."

March nodded affirmatively.

It was getting late. The morning would soon chase the darkness of the night into a memory. As tired as they were, the adventure continued and the heat of the conversation kept them awake. Too interested in the next morsel. Sleep, that will be later.

Chapter 7

The tragic war was over. The curtain of events left behind was slowly lifting. The horror it revealed to the world was shocking in most cases, accepted by some and glorified by others.

Many had felt the Second World War was a necessary evil. The people who were directly involved as well as the world looking into the play-by-play through newspapers, movie news, and radio felt they too, were part of the action fighting for world peace and to rid the world of the axis powers.

The world had changed, and 1945 was the start of a new era. Franklin Roosevelt was dead, Harry Truman was president and the atomic bomb was dropped on Japanese cities on August 6th 1945 and August 9th 1945. The war ends. The American economic system shifts gears again. The voids caused by the war had created deep hunger in the world, much was needed and a great sense of urgency prevailed.

Chapter 8

"Our situation remained static, Gill. Same old shit."

"SOS, hey March? No money? Your father still out of work?"

"You got it right again, old pal. No money, living in the basement apartment with the roaches and water bugs. I was almost twelve when World War II ended. Life was bleak for many families. The factories had to re-tool for peacetime production. The job market was not fully able to absorb all the military people let out of service, the housing industry was just starting to produce much needed housing for all the people returning to civilization life. It was a perilous period for a few months."

"I remember those times March, but it wasn't long. Just a few months and the good times started to roll again. Cars started coming off the assembly lines and demand was higher than supply. If you wanted a car, the dealer hit you with a cash add on."

"That's right Gill. Sometimes as much as a thousand dollars on a two thousand dollar car.

People were working, Europe was rebuilding. My father had a job offer, a factory in Ellenville."

"That's in the Catskills, the Borscht Belt?"

"Right again Gill. The Catskills about ninety miles from New York City. We moved there and I went to high school in Ellenville."

"   And that's where you worked in the factory, your father worked there also?"

March nodded and continued the narrative. "That's right, I worked the hotel circuit with Joe."

Gill smiled. "Joe the cutter. What made the Catskills so popular?"

"The heat, the humidity of New York City. Don't forget in the summer there was no air conditioning. Most people in New York lived in apartments and the kids played in the streets or went to summer camps. They were away from their parents. The Borscht Belt was the ideal place to spend the summer. Easy to get to by car or by bus, only a two to three hour drive from New York."

"Still a good place to go now?"

"No, that was fifty, sixty years ago, Gill. Today it's a shit hole. Buildings in decay, most of the

61

hotels are in ruin or closed. The airline industry, the cruise line industry, air conditioning, television all killed the Catskills and the Pocono mountains as a vacation spot. Next it's the moon or mars!"

"Television, that's the big thing today?"

"Movies, DVDs, iPods, the European market, the Asian market, everything is different, everything is new."

"What happened with Joe the cutter? Gill asked.

We worked all summer, the summer of 1953. Then I met this Richard Kanshitt."

"Richard Can-shit?"

"Kanshitt, Kanshitt" I do the jokes wise guy."

Gill smiled and nodded to March.

"Yeah, go on."

"So after the summer was over and I graduated from high school, Richard and I decided we needed to travel, so we took a trip. Canada and Alaska and to see America by car.

"In your used Pontiac?"

"Yep. One day Richard says to me 'let's take a ride.' And I said 'Where do you want to go'? He shrugs his shoulders because he doesn't know and he doesn't care. So with about fifteen dollars between us we head out to see the world."

"No money?"

"We worked. We picked beans, string beans in North Carolina, peaches in Georgia, corn in Iowa, potatoes in Idaho, we were paid by the pound and we were paid every day. We slept in the car or in some ladies house, or with a lady we picked up at some bar or with anyone and anything. Just two bums having a free life style; day laborers in a world of adventure."

"With no money?"

"Yeah with no money. Richard worked for two days in a garage, I worked in a diner washing dishes for one day, one day as a loader… Anything to put gas in the tank and then it was off to the next town then the next state."

"Did you guys ever get into real trouble?"

"Did we?! One day we got into it with three guys; just for the hell of it. Well one of the guys takes off his shoe and puts it on his hand like a glove, and he hits Richard in the mouth. He split Richard's lip. Very painful. I took a tire iron from the Pontiac and went after the bum, he ducks and hits me in the stomach, I bend over and he hits me in the chin."

"Good fighter!"

"Oh yeah, except then I fell on my ass, and hit my head on the ground. I grabbed Richard and ran, headed for some town, who knows where we were, some bar someplace.

Chapter 9

"America the beautiful, truly Gods land. North to Alaska, then to Canada, then to Brooklyn. We lived with Richard Kanshitt's father, I slept on the couch. Richard had a bunch of friends continuously from the time he was in kindergarten. In as much as they lived in the same neighborhood, they all were involved in some kind of shady transactions."

"Crime?"

"Yeah, teenage gangsters entangled in some kind of trouble."

"Go on."

"Well, one night we get a phone call, Richard's father had a phone in the apartment."

"Go on."

"Black hat, one of Richard's gangster friends, wants to go for a ride. We just swiped a Buick, I think it was almost new. So we went for a ride at 11:30 at night, in a very 'hot' car. They let me drive, there were five of us.

'Come on, go, go!' they shouted, so I hit the

gas and we were flying low."

"No stopping for red lights?"

"No, we just were going. Past everything, cars, trucks, ambulances, everything."

"Not worried, what could stop you?"

"Nothing, at that age! We were unstoppable gods of the road, invincible!"

"In a stolen car?"

"Yes."

"The wild bunch, and you were driving?"

"Yes."

"Any remorse?"

"Not then, Gill."

"They stopped you of course?"

"Yes, I passed a police car. I was going too fast to stop, went right past him."

"You stopped of course?"

"I sure did, there were two cops in the car, guns pointed at us. In about five minutes there were more police cars, and then another one."

"Off to jail with you!"

"They took us to the lock-up on Rikers Island, in the East River near Queens."

"Lovely, you are now a booked felon!"

"No."

"How come no?"

"Well it was early in the morning, almost day light. They shoved all of us into a large holding cell, filled with other prisoners of all ages."

"So?"

"Well I guess it was clean-up time. A guard with a large hose, like a fire hose washed down the cell floor, and some of us too."

"So?"

"One of the guys I was with slipped on the smooth concrete floor."

"Yeah, so?"

March looked very sad. "He cracked his head. It was all bloody and oozing."

"I'm sorry." Said Gill, lowering his eyes. *What a mess this guy gets into. But it makes good copy, I hope.* "Go on."

"Well two guards came into the compound, about six stood behind the bars with guns, just in case. They carried off the boy in a stretcher. Then they opened the gate and told everyone to get out, leave, and go home. We walked back to Brooklyn, it took us all day."

"No shoes?"

"We had shoes, but they took our shoe laces. Very uncomfortable walk."

Chapter 10

Life was uneventful for March Krantz. In his late teens, almost twenty now, he had no expertise in any field or financial experience. No income and no activity that had any direction. He was alone in the world, surrounded by his inept condition he created by lack of enthusiasm and foresight for things to come. He had not even acknowledged what was in front of him, his life to come, or his future and ability to provide for himself. So drifting in an aimless mode of nothing, he went back to Ellenville to try again to live with his parents, who afforded him nothing and in return asked for nothing and received the same: nothing.

Richard Kanshitt had met a girl, he was in love. March tried to talk him out of it. He told him all girls were the same. They all tickled you under the balls. They all looked great, though some of them he knew looked terrible.

"So, don't hook up with a girl. Stay with me and have fun! No future necessary."

But Richard wanted the girl and March couldn't talk

him out of it. So he married her and March was all alone.

Back to Ellenville. Maybe he would find what he wanted living with his parents; if he knew what he wanted. Back to work in the hotels, back to the comic routine, a procedure that was comfortable for him.

March had the same submissive desperation that most people his age had toward their parents. He wanted direction, he wanted guidance. Times were tough for them all. There was no mental firmness. Life was brutal, vigorous, and overly aggressive. In addition his mother, Anna, was a mental case, going to a doctor for nerves. There was no emotional stability and in addition she went to a clinic bi-monthly for electrical shock treatment. One of the doctors told her to take up smoking. He said it would "calm her nerves." Poor impoverished family.

Chapter 11

March remained in Ellenville for 2 months. He sold the Pontiac, gave his father almost all the money and bought a bus ticket for New York. He took a deep breath and left home with a small suitcase, and a large desire for something better. He did not know what he wanted or what he thought he needed. March arrived in New York City in June, hot sweaty June. He didn't have enough money for a hotel at New York City prices. So the first night he found a flop house, paid the two dollars and slept okay on a surplus army cot.

Time to look for a job, something, anything for money. He went to several job agencies he saw in a newspaper ad. No address to give them and no phone number to follow up.

"But you got a job anyway, March?"

"Sure lucky, I had only five dollars left. That night, the second, I slept on a park bench. Good old Central Park. It was chilly at night. A bum, hobo, I met at the park told me to put newspapers inside my shirt, it worked. Next day I went back to one of the agencies and they gave me an address to go to."

"You got a job!"

"My third day in New York I got a job.

"How?" said Grayson. "No address, no real experience except at bumming around and screwing, you sure are lucky. But how?"

"Well this guy I went to had a store on Madison Avenue and 59th Street. A small store and he needed a shipping clerk who would help clean and make deliveries and pick-up stuff he needed to fill orders."

"What kind of store?"

"A decorating store, you know, draperies, bedspreads, towels, handkerchiefs with monograms, that type."

"He accepted you without an address or anything? Why you could kill him, rob the store, steal all the merchandise and disappear!"

"You're going too far Gill, aren't you?"

"Just kidding March, go on."

"In a way you're right, but I told him the truth. Why I left home, my life up to that point and he believed me."

"How did you live, until you got your first pay?"

"I slept on the park bench. Ate garbage, raided garbage cans for scraps. Used the public bathrooms and survived."

"You had a lot of tendency to stick it out, didn't you?"

"I really had no choice. In my heart and soul I was on the right Avenue. Soon I was hoping I would come to the fork in the road that would lead me to some kind of life, some kind of success, even though I didn't know what I wanted. Just something more than a park bench. Lucky for me the park bench was a good task master."

"How?

"Sometimes, day or night, I had nothing to do so I wrote poems. I wrote lyrics, things, thoughts to keep my mind and soul together."

"Did the cops bother you, sleeping on a park bench?"

"In a way they helped me survive."

"Really, how was that, March?"

"I must have been the cleanest bum sleeping in Central Park, only because I was the newest bum. Anyway there was a cop, Danno, he made the rounds at night, kept everything peaceful. Bench life was tranquil when I was there."

"You were lucky you had a friend in blue, someone to keep you safe."

"Yes, he made his rounds and would tap his night stick on my shoes and tell me I can't sleep in the park, it's not safe, but then he would keep on walking and would come back about an hour later and tell me the same thing, tap my shoes or the bottom of my feet and keep on walking."

"How long did you sleep in the Central Park?"

"About five days. I got paid and looked for a furnished room. I found one in the Bronx that belonged to a divorced woman with a young boy. It was one bedroom so she doubled up with her son and I slept on the sofa. Not bad for twenty dollars a month. I stayed there about two months and then I moved to Brooklyn."

"Why?"

"I don't know, I guess I'm just used to Brooklyn. Don't forget I lived there until I was thirteen before we moved to Ellenville."

"So you worked in the store, learning to become a decorator?"

"Yes, in a way I did. The introduction was a blessing, a college degree, a great learning experience."

"So at last you were happy, you had somewhat of a home?"

"True, the owner was a transported Frenchman who spoke Spanish, French, English and some good old Brooklyn words from me and I learned a smatter of French from him. He was a good boss and a benefactor to me."

"How was that March?"

His brother in law was a prosperous business man, with too many suits and ties and stuff, so I was the recipient of the overstock. Boy I sure needed the help."

"That's the silk stocking district of New York!"

"Yes, I met a lot of very, very, important people. The Barcades from Barcada Rum. The Madora family, they owned a large shipping company, the Rockefellers, I did work in their Fifth Avenue apartment. From what I remember it was two floors. Wood paneled walls all over the place. You pushed at a point in the wall and a door opened. Many, many rooms, many doors."

"Nice people to do business with March?"

"It was my fault. One of the work men put his dirty jacket on her bed, it was a beautiful bedspread and boy was she mad, she really let me have it."

"Happy Rockefeller?"

"She wasn't happy then, she wanted to take ten percent off the bill. I cried poverty, I told Happy Rockefeller my boss would fire me, there wasn't enough money in the job to begin with and we gave it away so we could say we did work for the Rockefellers."

"She went for it?"

"Yes, she did. Ten percent of six thousand dollar job is six hundred! I wasn't going to let six hundred dollars go, just like that."

"You're a fighter, March."

"A street fighter Gill, with teeth and claws."

I guess you have to be to live your life!"

"My life has always been a conflict, an attempt to survive, but so has it been for most people. It seems that you have to learn to fight, or at least give the impression of a fighter, or you get lost in the parade. Paralysis sets in and you spend your life in a mental freeze needing the help of others or you perish. You're wiped out or destroyed and you did it yourself. It makes me think back to my parents, my mother.

I was about nineteen, my buddy Kanshitt had a pal whose father had a trucking company with a fleet of semis. He had a contract to haul frozen chickens to New York from Livingston Manor, about 30 miles north of Ellenville. His son Bill needed company for the drive into New York and he asked me to ride with him. Bill showed me how to drive the truck but didn't really teach me, so when his father asked me if I wanted a job as a driver I said okay. There I was, a truck driver."

"My God, and you knew nothing?"

"A tiny little bit, I managed to get the monster

going. The problem was my age as well as my inexperience. Bill told his father to give me a job, no one asked my age or my knowledge of driving an eighteen wheeler. No one checked anything. Later I found out you have to be twenty-five to be insured with the company and you needed a trucker's license. Here I was, no permission, deviated from the law and certainly out of my range of knowledge."

"Scared?"

"No, more stupid than scared and I did it, I drove for three months that summer, until the controller asked for my license."

"You were cooked."

"Cooked and served on a platter head first, good bye trucking job."

"How much did they pay you to wreck their company?"

"Seventy a week, but there's more."

"Oh, do tell."

"I drove to New York, Brooklyn, and Utica Avenue and they unhooked my box."

"Box, you mean the trailer."

"Get with it Gill, it's a box."

"Okay the box. Tell me about it."

"They unhooked the box and gave me a new empty one to take back to the company."

"No frozen chickens?"

"No it was empty. There was a man who was hanging around the wholesale food market all the time. I pulled into the dock to unload. One time he walks up to me and asks me if I want to make some extra money. I told him I'll listen, so we went to get a drink and he told me he was part owner of a cleaning service."

"Sounds like a gangster to me."

"No it's almost on the up and up. What they did was contract with the camps in the Catskills. They would pick up the footlockers with the kids dirty laundry and deliver the lockers to their homes. Then the mothers or maids would wash the stuff and put it back in the footlockers. So then the trucks would pick them up and return them to the kids."

"So where did you fit March?"

"Well the guy asks me if I would deliver the lockers to a pickup point, the clean clothes lockers!"

"How much?"

"Dollar twenty five cents each locker."

"How many could you get in your truck, excuse me your box?"

"About two to three hundred."

"My God, that's about three hundred a week."

"Plus my salary."

"You spent it, every cent?"

"In a way, yes. I had to buy extra fuel for the truck and stuff like that."

"Stuff like what?"

"My boss."

"Bill's dad?"

"Yes."

"Go on."

"He found out I was hauling clothes lockers on the side."

"You got fired?"

"No, he just wanted one hundred a week to pay toward my use of the rig. He told me most of his drivers were doing the same thing."

"Cash money, of course."

"Always cash money."

"The rest of it, spent on wine, women and song?"

"Yes, something like that." March shrugs his shoulders. "I've always been carefree with money." His expressing indifference was due to his upbringing. He never had any, and didn't know how to use it when he got some. You had to be taught and disciplined to understand daily social interaction and reciprocal actions.

Chapter 12

Back to work, March enjoyed living in Brooklyn. The fifty dollars a week from his job paid his rent and gave him enough to eat like a normal person, no garbage can menus. The money was just enough to have little extra for some sort of a limited social life.

"So, you moved to Brooklyn, where?"

"I got a furnished room in a brownstone type house, in the basement for twenty-five dollars a month." March reminisced.

"Sounds good March, indoor living."

"Except it was a real dump. Roaches and water bugs all over the place. I guess they come with me. My crawling pets."

"Where was this palace?"

"In Brooklyn, in Brighton. I guess we are used to places we come from. I felt comfortable there."

"Some of us do, some of us try to live better than that. I guess fifty dollars a week and that's a good life?" Grayson was incredulous.

"All I could do at the time. It was okay with me. I had peace and quiet, no screaming, and my own place to sleep, my own bed and a radio. Plus the Boardwalk was just a few blocks away. To me all this was marvelous."

"Life had intrinsic value at long last, hey March?"

"Yeah, a place to rest my head and a job, a real job. I felt distinguished, ingenious, and part of the superior human race."

"I understand and I feel good for you. Go on."

"I was working at the store, decorating studio, whatever you want to call it. It had been about a year, when one day I was alone in the store and a man comes in. He looks around and stares at me, nothing said, just stares. He had a sorrowful face, big man, well dressed but nothing said. I looked him in the eyes and nodded at him as a sign of greeting. Nothing said, he just looked at me. I thought he was there to rob the store. I don't know why I just felt that way. He kept starring. A chill ran through me. It must have been more than a minute before he spoke."

"The boss sent me." He spoke with a slight accent, maybe Sicilian, maybe Sardinian?"

"Some place in Italy? Right March?"

"Sure sounded Italian to me!"

"The speech expert. Go on speech doctor."

"Sure was glad he wasn't going to rob or kill me."

"That bad looking?"

"Yes scary type. I kept looking at him.

"Who's the boss?" March asked him. He replied

"You'll meet him. Look you don't have to come. I was told to ask you, not force you to come to see him. Do you want to go? I'll pick you up after work."

I was very confused. "What's his name, and who are you?" I asked him. I was very soft spoken, he didn't look like the type of person you wanted to have for anything but a friend.

"The boss is Joe Banorluga, you worked for his brother, Tony."

"Oh, the Naponach Country Club! That was

almost two years ago!"

"We know that"

"Whoa, whoa, how come you knew where to find me?"

"The boss keeps tabs on people."

"Just like the FBI?" I said.

He cracked a half smile. "Yeah, just like the FBI."

"So okay, pick me up after work." I said.

I met him at the parking garage on 59th street. He drove a new Desoto and his name was Herman.

"Brooklyn, East New York." He said. "Ozone Park near Pitkin Ave."

The ride from work in Manhattan took about an hour. The man didn't talk, if you asked him anything he would grunt or shrug. I don't think he liked conversation, and as time went by and I got to know him a little more, I realized he didn't like people. The perfect employee for Joe Banorluga. He parked the car in front of an old, old building, maybe over a hundred years old. It looked like it was made of bricks, but you could see the white wash plaster was starting to peel off the bricks and stone. A large building one story, and the neighborhood was old and dirty, not cared for at all. It was a bar, a saloon and as we went inside the smell of the whiskey rushed swiftly at us, a sudden attack of our senses. There were three men sitting at the bar, old men and old drunks. It was dinner time, not drinking time and I wanted to turn around and walk out. Then I thought *how would I get home? And where am I?* Too many thoughts going through my head. Why was I here, what do I do, and why was I kidnapped to Ozone Park, near Pitkin Avenue.

It was a large room, almost the size of a movie theater. The theater of the absurd. The darkness was broken by a small lamp over the bar and half lit ceiling lights high above us. Herman looked at March for a few seconds and signaled him to follow by cocking his head. March followed Herman, moving slowly so he wouldn't bump into anything. It was more than a little scary. If he didn't know Tony,

Joe's brother, he would have walked out and found

a way to get home. Curiosity owned him now. They walked toward the back of the building, somehow Herman knew the way in the near darkness. March could see illumination reflecting under the door they were approaching, a few more steps and he could smell cigar smoke.

The door opened to a large living room, lounge chairs, a bar, television, a large black leather sofa and three large men. Very surprising March thought, but not out loud. Three more large men were sitting in the lounge chairs and a seventh seated behind a beautiful black lacquer desk. The seventh man stood up, came forward from the desk and approached March wearing a great big smile.

"Hello pizino! Tony told me about you, I'm very happy you're here." They shook hands. Joe was very well dressed in a brown suit. A tall man, well over six feet and good looking with dark black hair thick and natural. It was the Italian look.

"Sit down, I'll tell you why I asked you to come." He extended his hand toward an empty chair. "Sorry about Herman, he's my driver. Herman looks like death warmed up. Scary person, but he wouldn't hurt a fly."

Laughter from the other men. Someone yelled

out, "You should be a fly!" Joe Banorluga's face changed. It was someone who changed from an angel to the devil himself, in seconds. March noticed the anger molded his looks. He didn't look like the man who shook hands ten seconds ago. His face was red, his lips tight, his fists clenched and he seemed to stand on his toes. He looked at the intruder with knives in his eyes. The man with the big mouth and smart remark lowered his head. Joe's gaze turned to March.

"Sorry about that." His gaze now on the man with the remark. March thought Joe Banorluga could turn water into ice by looking at it, and now he was very scared.

The angelic look was back. "Look March, the reason you're here is simple math. Liquor times people equals money."

March was confused, what the hell was Joe talking about? And why the outburst? He just stood befuddled, nothing to say now, just to listen.

Joe continued. "I was told you're a very funny young man, very entertaining, and very amusing. That's right, isn't it?"

March still didn't know what was going on. He shook his head and continued to listen.

"My brother said you…" pointing at March, "…could put on a show. Am I right?"

March again shook his head, not knowing what he was getting himself into.

Joe went on. "See this place?" He pointed at the closed door. March again shook his head. A small nod, yes. "This place it's too big. It needs to become something. A money maker, right now it's a money taker. I need you…" Again pointing at March, "…to create a night club, a showplace for me! Can you do it? Capish?"

March nodded yes again, not knowing why or what was happening.

Joe Banorluga resumed is narrative. "I own eleven old, run-down buildings like this one. They're all over the place. New York, Connecticut, New Jersey, Pennsylvania, all over the place. Oh yeah, Boston also. Can you turn them into money machines for me?"

March finally got it, but how was he going to do what Joe wanted and why? "Joe, I'm still in diapers! I don't know anything about construction or night clubs. Anything you want me to do is out of my realm of knowledge."

Joe was pacing the room now, his hand holding his chin as he walked and thought. "You're getting this all wrong my boy. I don't need you to paint, hammer nails, or be an architect. I want you…" Pointing again, "…to be the showman. The guy you were at my brothers joint. Sure you can help with the design, work with the builders, pick out the paint colors, but your main deal is to put on shows. Make it good shows so crowds will come in see and to spend. Remember what I just said? "Liquor times people equals money."

March was thinking. He could do this. He did it before, by an accidental occurrence, and this could be a planned adventure. Maybe this is the fork in the road, the direction he should take; the direction he was looking for. He looked at Joe, jumped up from the chair, and walked over to Joe Banorluga to shake his hand.

"Wow." Joe said in an exclamation of surprise. If all my lungs had your enthusiasm life would really jell for me. Let's go March!"

"Do I have to quit my job?"

"No, no, no March, never quit. You'll need the front, I'm paying you in cash. The job will cover how you live, pay taxes, and it's a good front. Keep your job."

"Will I have time for both?"

"No not really. There will be times when you work your ass off, you're ready to quit, but don't. And don't cross me and don't cross your boss in the store, just keep going.

Chapter 13

March had extra money now. The money Joe Banorluga gave him covered his expenses and his extras as needed and almost seventy to two hundred a month left over, but he was working his ass off. Night and day. Daytime at the store, night time at the club. Working with the architect, the contractors, the painters, getting everything just right. Joe would buy the empty building next to the club and have it bulldozed so the club would have parking. Joe and March made a good team. Two forward thinkers, two visionary minds. The club was nearly completed and the kitchen was installed with new equipment; the best available at any price. March supervised the sound system and the lights for the stage and seating area. Joe Banorluga wanted the club to work. His name and his reputation were up front. There was no reprimand from the outside world and he didn't take reputes. His way was all or nothing. It was life or death, no gray just black and white.

March Krantz wrote the material needed for the nightclub show. He wrote the lyrics for the songs and hired the bands, girls, and acts. Joe was amazed at his natural talent and untrained knowledge. He had perceived enlightenment of the job. They needed a name for the club, and since no one could think of one they liked, they held a contest. Joe put an ad in the New York Daily Mirror saying 'Name our new club and get a week in Florida.' It was all expense paid with two hundred in cash a week at the Fountain head hotel. March and Joe came up with idea together for publicity. The final name, Lights Out. It was won by a dancer named Janet. March gave her a top billing spot in the show. It took almost six months for the word to get around and the crowds to come, but come they did. March was on top of the world. Another dollar or thousand for all. Joe Banorluga was making the money he wanted and the club was always packed with a waiting line around the block.

Chapter 14

"Hello folks, you should have seen me last month. Boy was I fat." Krantz the skinny kid, dressed in a tux was on stage. The eight o'clock show; one of three that he did each night.

"Hello folks, how do I look? Man you should have seen me last month, boy was I fat. I had my stomach lubricated twice a day so I could squeeze into my car. You know I bought a new car, power brakes, power windows and power payments! It has an imported economy engine so tremendous fuel savings but it's a little slow. Zero to sixty in four hours. Downhill! This is a terrible situation. You go out and pay a load of money for products you buy today and everything is defective. My friend just bought a new water bed and a swimming pool together. People don't care about the things they do anymore. Nothing is made to last and nobody signs their work. Who cares anyhow, why I just bought a new painting and it was so bad I hung the artist…"

The show had a schedule of two hours,

however the audience's overzealous association prolonged the time March had to spend on stage. He didn't mind, he enjoyed the outbursts and had a comeback for anything the crowd would throw at him. He told a heckler, "God told you to come forth. He has your brains, but you came fifth!"

A drunk one night was uttering profanities at March. He told the driver, "Nice to see you again! You were here last week! By the way where is that beautiful blonde I saw you with last time?" The woman he was with took it seriously and started causing a scene. The club bouncers, Joe Banorluga's thugs, escorted them both out of the room by their necks and out the back door of the club into the alley. The woman resisted and the two goon bouncers held her arm. They pushed her down to the ground and broke her arm. Joe Banorluga had to pay off the cops. He didn't want another incident to administrate, his plate was full. So Joe sent Leo, one if his brothers, to the couple's home. Leo told them any more actions by the two of them and they'll have more than a broken arm. He pulled a gun out of his shoulder holster and pointed at the man's stomach.

"Get me? Understood?" The man was white with terror and the wife already on the verge of hysteria. Nothing more was made of the occurrence.

Chapter 15

The Lights Out club had now open for over a year. It stayed open seven days a week, open from seven at night till sun up the next day. The crowds were there to support the long hours. March did three shows a night. One at eight, ten, twelve and sometimes two am. The eight o'clock show was the only one that started on time. The following shows were always late because they ran overtime and bumped each other; pushing the time forward late into the night. The club had to close at two in the morning because of the liquor laws of New York City. To get around the laws the club sold memberships and became private. They invented a way to circumvent the law. For five dollars they gave you a pass and you were a member of their private club. They set-up your table with ice and sold hard liquor or beer at three dollars a glass; over the regular price. March would do a regular show for the club group and the girl dancers would do a strip tease. It worked well for Joe Banorluga. Extra money and extra acclaim for the crowd. The detectives from the 36th precinct near by the club got in for free. They all had a tab at the club, but never paid the bill. Joe understood how protection worked. His entire organization was based on threats of violence, including the eleven buildings he owned and many more he never talked about. The gangster real estate business. Lend money, more than they could pay back, and use the leverage to take over the indebted. It was loan sharking at its finest.

The years had been good for Joe Banorluga and his five brothers. They operated any way they wanted. No public outcry, no real effort to stop the organization and no police interference at that time. With almost five hundred operators, called soldiers, on the payroll. Some of them were full time, some part time to be called when needed.

A very impressive amount of money was allocated to advertising or local newspapers that lowers the adverse diplomacy; it kept the mob in good spirits with the public, except those who had to deal directly with them.

The Banorlugas had acquired wealth through property. They owned or had a controlling interest in many businesses, wholesale food, garbage collection, dry cleaners, fast food stores, broadcasting,

Seventh Avenue clothing manufacturing and distribution, money lending, and liquor distribution to hotels, night clubs, stores and restaurants. The cream of business in New York City and New York State. They also had many controlling interests in Connecticut, New Jersey, Massachusetts, Rhode Island and Pennsylvania, plus corporate control in many firms in Maryland and Delaware. Joe Banorluga had created a spider web of controls over his empire. Everyone took orders and reported to the person above themselves. Orders were followed without question and carried out exactly as given, or else. No one left the line-up and those who wanted to quit disappeared; on occasion their families followed.

The daily operation was the work and genius of Royal Samson. A remarkable talent with an ability for detail and follow through; the brain that makes things happen. Royal Sampson graduated from Princeton University in New Jersey with a doctorate in mathematics and calculus. He was the recipient of a formidable memory in addition to his other attributes. Joe Banorluga and Royal Samson went to school together from kindergarten on. They lived near the same public school in Brooklyn and had been friends and juvenile delinquents through high school. Joe's family had a home near Rockaway Avenue and Royal's family lived in an apartment close by, in Brownsville. Royal Samson's name in school was Larry Levine. Joe wanted no part of a Jewish association and compelled Larry to change his name. So he became Royal Samson. Joe always had a flair for the ridiculous and Royal Samson was enough of a rejuvenation to satisfy his outlandish nature.

"So Larry becomes Royal?"

Gill Grayson was thrilled with all the stories, enough to fill his pockets with material for a magazine article. "Let the progression continue." he said.

"Fuck you Gill, it's 4:30 in the morning! I'm going to bed."

So they retired for the night that was left.

Chapter 16

The cold of the morning was being chased by the warmth of the winter sun. Slowly, everything was stirring and waking up to the new day; including Gill Grayson. Gill dressed and headed for the kitchen. March was drinking his second cup of coffee.

"Morning, sleepy head. Want a cup?"

Gill nodded approval. They finished their coffee in silence. "Want to go for a walk?" asked March.

"Sure do, get the stiffness out of my bones."

"Old bones?"

Gill nodded again. "For sure. Let's go."

They bundled up and went into the snow. The weather was crisp and invigorating. A little brisk, but after all it was Connecticut in the winter. Tracks in the snow near the house told a story of animals in the region; mainly deer. The air smelled of winter flowers and tree sap, it was a sweet and delightful winter green morning. The forest surrounds the house with six acres of trees, trees and more trees;

101

mainly white birch. They walked about a half hour when March said he had enough cold fresh air. It was hard walking in the knee high snow. Back to hot coffee and warmth. They entered the mud room, took off their boots and headed for the study and plush armchairs.

The house was built in the nineteen sixties with lumber, brick, and love. Two stories high, March slept in the downstairs bedrooms; the maid's room. There were two of them, but he didn't like the empty feeling when he was on the second floor. Besides the staircase at his age was similar to climbing a mountain. The furnishings were colonial country, the same as the house. March had bought the home from an executive in the Cold War defense industry who had it built for his wife and the executive as a second home. March hired a top New York decorator and she stayed in the house with March for several weeks; decorating March and the house. The comfort and quiet of it all was good for day dreaming, composing, and tranquility. A spot of serenity in an insane world. March was also a poet, and thought about a poem he wrote when he first acquired his Connecticut home.

The summer air is everywhere

The trees with fruit are blooming

The bugs are crawling here and there

While flying things go zooming

The blue sky hovers above

A greening world of peace and love

If you listen, it need not be too clear

You can hear the whisper of the brook
so near

But don't listen too close or things

Remote you will hear.

There is man about now, we can hear
his footsteps   too and like he's done
before he's chopping down

The trees to get a better view

For he's building a house to escape

The summer breeze

And while he chops down the trees

He says he loves the woods and the
summer green,

And he keeps right on chopping trees

To escape the summer breeze.

Chapter 17

A great human this Joe Banorluga!"

"You don't know the half of it Gill."

"Go on March."

"Joe Banorluga's father Gessepie was an expert mason, a stone cutter in great demand. He came to the United States at the turn of the century."

"So, go on, who told you about Gessepie?"

"Joe and I were friends. We talked about everything, except his connection to the Cosa Nosta."

"Ok go on."

"So Gessepie was working with one of his brothers in Manhattan, a new high rise. They had borrowed money from the mob and the mob wanted it back."

"Go on."

"They sent one of their torpedoes to the job site to collect once the money was long overdue. Gessepie's brother got into a hustle and the torpedo pushed the brother off the roof. Gessepie was in shock, he couldn't move. The torpedo ran away. Gessepie had connections with the mob and found the torpedo. Once he did he choked the man slowly to death with a wire garret he made. The man was bigger than Gessepie but he was in a rage, nothing could stop him. After that Gessepie joined the gang, with the intent to kill each one of them. But something happened to Gessepie, he was making very good money and he liked being a torpedo, a soldier for the Black Hand, murder incorporated. He flourished, became a strong man and a leader. He had his own group who answered to him only. The years went by and his entourage grew. Eventually he formed his own mob, paid the soldiers well and lavished gifts on all his people. Cars, houses, whatever it took to hold the gang together. They were reckless and careless and pushed back at anyone and everything in their way. Soon they were the big boys of New York. The gang to be feared.

Joe's father did not live like a don. His life was simple, devoted to his organization, his mob family and their welfare. The First World War dug a deep hole into his gang. Most of his men were drafted or enlisted in to the service. Most of them had family roots in Europe and they wanted to help defeat the Germans. They enlisted into the armies of Free

Fighters and since they all were excellent soldiers none were killed. Five of them were wounded and came home unable to work. Gessepie took care of their family and all their needs. It was his honor to do that for his men."

"Strange properties considering they would kill without malice or thought!"

"Yes lots of malice Gill, they took money to accomplish anything anybody wanted. Dollars were their game plan. Money their roadmap."

"I see March, go on."

"They bought off elected officials in nine east coast states. Those they couldn't buy, the gang would threaten, and if they weren't able to convince danger or malice they went to the next step."

"What was that?"

"Car bombings, kidnapping, broken limbs, any threat was considered if the take was ample enough."

"Didn't the cops retaliate? Where was the F.B.I?"

"Everyone was chasing every one. It was a war within a war. Dillinger, Baby Face Nelson, Bonnie

& Clyde, Machine Gun Kelley,

Al Capone… Should I go on?"

"The F.B.I. what about the G men?"

"A small new group at that time, a work in progress. Not ready to take on all the troubles of the cities. America was forming a new child on the block. Soon we would come in to the forefront, but not yet. The liquor laws and the eighteenth amendment were passed in January, 1919. As I said we were the new kid on the block. Soon we would be able to stand up, but not yet."

"I remember Gessepie Banorluga's campaign in the thirties. He tried running for mayor of New York, isn't that right March?"

"Yes, he had too much money. The organization was tuned up to run by special motion. The gang had acquired a life of its own and was run by directives. Gessepie was getting old and tired and he wanted to retire; sort of retire. Maybe find a new life for himself? Most of his family had passed and his wife left him because of his involvements. So he was tired, and very, very rich. At this point competition was starting to cut into his slice of the pie. The new gangs were together in action and motive. They were run like large corporations with organization charts, building permits, and paid taxes. They looked like legitimate enterprise from a distance, and no outsider could get close enough to prove otherwise.

Gessepie had five children, all boys, all strong, tall and handsome, but only one excelled and was close to his father; the oldest Joe. Joe was the kingpin of the mafia. He was the strong man: the catalyst between his father and the mob of over a hundred people in the crime family. When he was seventeen he was working shoulder to shoulder with his dad. He often went on field trips with the boys. He held the baseball bat, sometimes using it himself just to show the men he wasn't afraid to get his hands dirty; and bloody. He was involved in murder, torture, kidnapping and anything the boys and his dad thought was necessary to maintain the family business. It wasn't only men on the mob's payroll. They had eight women who were just as ruthless as the men. They were all just as tough and determined as the men, not emotional, not sentimental, very brutal, and very violent. They were similar to the Kali of India, they murdered and maimed in the service of the mob. You borrowed and you paid back. One way or the other.

The Banorluga's were church goers. Gessepie went to church in the old country. His father went to church, his grandfather went to church so Gessepie's family went to church. He insisted, no way out, you didn't miss a service, you just went. So Joe's family went to church. It was just the right thing to do. Kill and repent. The Banorluga's fit into the community as much as possible. They gave money to the schools, to the church, they even owned a hospital on Kings Highway in Flatbush where they paid employees above union scale. Most of the patients were not charged, a community thing and a tax write off; great publicity.

As Joe became older, in to his late teens, he took on responsibility for running the whole system. His father was on the outside, Joe was the inner control. However it was getting too big for one person. Joe asked for his long time buddy, Larry Levine a.k.a. Royal Samson to help maintain the organization. Royal had a job working part time and going to Princeton during the day. Joe offered him a huge sum of money to get involved with the boys, plus a salary of fifty thousand a year. An offer he could not refuse. The pudgy Royal was looking forward to using his doctorate to become a professor one day, but in his mind this was adventure, excitement, sex, and control. No more small stature, behind the front line he would be in control, second in command, a big man. His ego swelled at the idea. The law, morals, and family relations were on the sidelines. He was taken over with his new adventure, poor Royal. Gessepie told Joe and Royal the rules of the game. Money lending, prostitution, protection, and most all liquor sales, that was their game plan. No drugs! He didn't want to import from South America or Cuba. He didn't trust those people and he didn't need them. The game board was designed and played by the Banorlugas, they didn't want anyone controlling their actions or telling them when their stuff is ready. They were controlling the factors and they alone ran the sequence of events.

The big cities were the playgrounds of the mobs. Chicago and New York because of their large populations were ideal fields of cash for the families. This wasn't enough for them, they were looking west to Los Angeles and Las Vegas. There was trouble in Los Angeles. March 1931 was the year of the Sheldon and Frank kidnapping and Zeke Careas shooting a policeman. Tony and Frank Cornero were the leading wholesalers of bootleg liquor in Southern California. James "well fed" Murphy and Joseph "cockeye" Herring were just a few of the hoods wounded. Max Silver was killed as well as Domino Dicioll.

Joe and his father wanted no part of California

after the news was received. They were right on target, no pun intended. In the nineteen forties Mickey Cohen was wounded in his right shoulder by a shotgun blast. They remained where they were, well entrenched in their business. Things were just swell Joe told his people. 'Don't leave anything behind or the cops or feds could pin it on us.' And so things went on, money and power were building up, the city was more and more theirs as time went by."

"How did you know all the details March, you told me you and Joe talked but you said no details were given. That true?"

"Yes Gill, sort of. He didn't want me involved in anything that would bite me in the ass or fall back on him and his organization. Still the torpedoes in the clubs, the bartenders, the front men, the muscle men, even the women, they all talked, all the time. Don't you talk about your job?"

"I'm not working for the Banorluga family, March."

"True and if Joe knew you had a big mouth and were a danger to him he would get rid of you somehow."

"If he knew you were the mouth that roared?"

"Yeah well with so many people in the group, someone would find out."

"Anyone you knew?"

"Many years ago, in the far off land of Brooklyn, they found a body floating in the East River. It was a sloppy job. The paper told the story. The body had no tongue and its wrists were bound with wire. He had been burned, whipped and slashed. He should have been tied down with cinder blocks and dumped in the Atlantic."

"You knew the guy?"

"I think so, one of the bouncers in Joe's night club in Newark, New Jersey. I used to talk to him when I worked that club, but then I never saw him again."

"You were associated with him for many years?"

"Yes until I was about thirty five or so."

"He picked you up, out of the gutter."

"Yes he did, and he put clothes on my back as well as money in my pocket. For that and the trust in my work, I'm grateful to him."

113

"You were the young kid on the block with the controlling switch in your hand."

"Not really. I ran the nightclubs. At that time in the mid-fifties Joe had eight clubs. I controlled the talent and hired the performers. Nothing really mob related."

"A load of work for a man in his mid-twenties, wouldn't you say?"

"I loved doing it. It was exciting and rewarding. Joe backed me up on almost anything. He had the understanding and the will to make the clubs work, and they did."

"Plenty of talent in New York for you to hire?"

"Oh yes, oh literate one. Show girls, magicians, dancers of all types, musicians…" March leaned back. His eyes toward the ceiling thinking about the memories. "I even hired classical performers once in a while and had them do popular pieces. It went over well. We got write-ups in the papers. They were good reviews, comments from people in the business. It all increased the gate. Tons of money. Nightclubs were very popular in the fifties."

"What about food, did they serve food?"

"Oh yes, you could get a full steak dinner, just pay the price. Equal to about fifty buck today, but coffee or tea was included. So was ketchup and a glass of water."

"You're very funny March."

"I'm told that once in a while. Isn't that why you are here, Gill?"

"Oh, go on wise guy."

"Of course you could order Chinese food. \A meal cost five dollars per person, everything included."

"Good food March?"

"Not bad, very expensive. Chinese in a good restaurant would be about three dollars, tip included."

"Made to your order?"

"Oh know Gill, pre-cooked, served from a set menu, no deviations. A large pot of chow mein was cooked every night with all the supplemental items that accompany the dinner, and it was plenty of food, more than most people could or want to eat. It justifies the price, maybe."

"Lots of leftover food to feed the rats?"

115

"Not the rats, Gill the people. The leftover Chinese went back into the big pots. Joe said it was too expensive to throw out food and have garbage trucks, which he owned, haul it away. His excuse was to protect the landfills."

"Good God, March, didn't the food inspectors catch any of this?"

"Yes, but who had the balls to challenge Joe Banorluga?"

"I'm not going to eat out anymore."

"No one died from our food. Other things sure, but not the food!"

"Keep the prices high, and the overhead low?"

"Course, we were there to make money. People who went to night clubs could afford the prices. You should have seen the cars parked near the club. Buicks, Cadillacs, Rolls, Chrysler New Yorkers, everything. Nothing cheap about the crowds."

"No television?"

"Yes, TV was alive and starting to roll, big time. Remember

Sid Caesar, Milton Berle? There was plenty to

watch, but people like to socialize. They like to get out, be with others, and spend money on dates, wives, and friends. Even though the movies were going and TV was around, night clubs were still strong in the fifties."

"And so was the gangster business, right March?"

"True, true and so was the gangster business, your right Gill. Joe Banorluga was still a young man, not yet twenty five in the mid-fifties. His father was laid back so Joe was the king pin. He was the go-to guy. Gessepie had many enemies he had accumulated over the years. People he cheated, people he killed, other mobs he had pushed aside and they all never forgot. Police were still working on cases they knew he was involved in or where Gessepie was the hit man. Many people did not look the other way, did not forget.

Captain Manny Schwartz was the commander at the 36th precinct, a few blocks from the Lights Out club. He had locked horns

With Gessepie Banorluga many times over the years. He knew the cruelty and the indifference to the suffering of others Gessepie displayed. He knew of cases that left children without a parent, people without hope, bankrupt, poverty, crippled, complete disregard for the human spirit and it affected him deeply. From what I understand his thoughts were consumed with the conviction of the Banorluga bunch and Gessepie Banorluga especially. He made it his life work to get them off the streets. To him The Boys in the Street were the creation of the devil. Captain Schwartz was in his late fifties, muscle turned to fat, hair thinning to nothing, clothes that needed cleaning, and liver that needed a rest from too much whiskey and a passion to get the

Banorluga family, even if it meant going outside the law and risking his badge and pension.

He was following a case that happened a few years ago in the Bronx. It looked like Gessepie's work, his style, his no care, fuck you attitude. A man owned a pizza shop in the Bathgate section of the Bronx. The business was good, he was ready to open a second shop with the money he had saved. He was going to buy a building instead of renting, but he needed a few thousand dollars more than he had. That's when the Banorlugas came into the picture. They had a small office in the Bronx near East Tremont Ave. It was a loan office, a money lending machine. Beautiful surroundings; a quiet, peaceful environment. Coffee and cookies were offered by a very attractive young lady. She looked like she was a school girl, but she was in her thirties. Pretty, nice, soft spoken and a friend to all. Mr. Pizza parlor man went to that office to borrow ten thousand dollars. The young lady, after his coffee and cookies explained to him the conditions of the loan. No collateral needed, just his signature on a promissory note. The payback would be for 36 months at two-hundred-seventy-seven dollars and eighty-eight cents per month and he would get the ten-thousand in cash. The note would be for sixteen thousand. There was an extra six thousand in interest taken out in advance, plus ninety dollar a month handling fee, also taken out of the loan in advance. Total monthly payment three hundred sixty seven dollars and eighty cents. Plus ten percent interest on the six thousand."

"It all sounds very complicated, March."

"Complicated and shady." March had been privy to hundreds of those deals. He knew exactly how they went down and could just imagine how it all went down with the pizza owner...

"Interest is another payment of $106." The attractive woman running the loan office said. "Is that okay Mr. Pizza Man?"

"When do I get my $10,000?"

"Today, right now." Just agree to pay back four hundred seventy three a month, okay?"

"Sure sounds okay to me."

"Good Mr. Pizza man, I'll get your money. Hundred dollar bills okay?"

Everything was okay at that moment in time. He built his store, did a great business and was able to pay the monthly payments with its high interest. A bank would have charged him about three hundred nineteen a month, but a bank wouldn't loan him anything.

Gessepie Banorluga had a nephew living in the Tremont area. The nephew, age sixteen, needed a job. A wild kid, never listened to anyone. He was a real trouble maker, a Banorluga kid.

Gessepie asked if he could get the kid a job. He drove to the Bronx with one of his torpedoes and asked, really told, Mr. Pizza man to give the kid a job. He told him what to pay the kid, and Mr. Pizza man said no.

Gessepie told him to hire the kid or he would call in the loan, demand all payment at once. The outstanding balance was over seven thousand. He told Gessepie there was no recall clause. This caused Gessepie to slap his face hard.

"Don't talk back to me!" he said. "Just listen. You didn't read the promissory note, did you?"

"No, it was too many pages."

"Of course it was, I know that, I wrote it. It says your real estate is collateral. As well as your car, your house, your furniture, everything."

"The girl in your office told me no collateral was needed!"

"She lied. Now hire my nephew, or give me your Pizza Parlor back with the buildings."

"Would you take the cash owed?"

"The interest is now twelve thousand plus the seven thousand five hundred you owe. Pay up now, or hire my nephew."

Those were his choices, so he hired the nephew, knowing the kid would be a hindrance. Sure enough, the nephew never did anything he was told. One day in the old pizza place, he was left alone for two hours. After ten o'clock he closed up and went home, leaving the pizza ovens on. They

overheated and one exploded. The building burnt to
the ground.

Chapter 18

March and Gill were in front of the house throwing snow balls at each other. One went down March's collar on his neck.

"That's enough fresh air, Gill, let's go inside." Back to the study and the warmth.

"March, I've always wondered about your name. It's unusual no?"

"Well my parents owed all the relatives money, everyone, dead and alive. Some recent, some going back many years. Who should they name me after? No one was safe from the handout, one dollar, five dollars, anybody, and anything. They needed a neutral name and I was born in March, so here I am."

"How interesting."

"You think it's interesting. I think it stinks. What a way to grow up."

"Lots of poor people in this country, March. Look at you now."

"Yeah, I know, I'm just shooting off my

123

mouth."

"Yes."

"Sorry, but you asked."

"Yes, that's why I'm here. Besides your hospitable time and lovely home, what more can I ask?"

"Want me to call over a couple of broads?"

"No thank you, just the interview."

"How long do we have? Another day, another week, how long?"

"I really don't know March. It's your story, your life, you tell me."

"I don't know."

"Just keep talking."

"Okay. Well when I was thirty one I met a wonderful woman, Elizabeth."

"Tell me about her."
"I am. I met her at a Nights of Columbus social. There were over a thousand people and I was the mc. I did some stand-up and had some singers do some of my song lyrics. It was fun night for

everyone."

"In New York?"

"New Rochelle. She lived in White Plains."

"You did quite a few social type meetings. Clubs, organizations, labor unions, groups, political campaigns, industry, business, lodges, fund raisers, right March?"

"Yes I did them all. Sometimes a complete show, everything. It was dependent on what they could afford."

"What determined that?"

"I asked them. Point blank, is two thousand okay, can you pay five thousand? Sometimes I didn't change anything, just my agent's fee of two hundred. Only I never had an agent, just me!"

"Work at the club, the store in Manhattan, the master of ceremonies, you were making a small fortune!"

"Not a large fortune."

"You're still working, still raking it in?"

"Yes, so, you want some of it, write your book."

"That's just what I'm doing."

"Good."

"Tell me more about Elizabeth."

"Sure. She was the treasurer of the Knight of Columbus lodge. She didn't book the show, the entertainment secretary did that. She paid the bills, me included, only she didn't want to write a check to me for six thousand. She wanted a typed invoice with my company name, an invoice number, address, the whole kettle of fish. Well I didn't want to do that. Joe taught me to forget the bullshit just get the money. I told miss smarty pants if I didn't get my check now, as arranged beforehand with the entertainment secretary, she would have to pay me an additional nine hundred. I had a paper to that effect. She wrote me the check and as she handed me the envelope, she told me to my face to choke on the check. Then she said, 'Party's over Mr. Krantz, go fuck off.' Imagine a broad saying that forty years ago."

"Gutsy type."

"Yes and smart. I was intrigued, she excited me. I was fascinated! I just had to see her again, but how?"

126

"Tell me."

"I waited a few days, and then I called the entertainment secretary. I asked him about coming events where he told me of a meeting in two months to nominate new officers. I didn't ask, I told him I would be there. He said no. I told the secretary Joe Banorluga was my friend, and he knew who he was and I got my invite. I sent him a hundred dollar bill to keep things cool."

"Throwing your weight around March?"

"Sometimes you have to. Anyway, I show up at the meeting early and she's not there. Want to see a grown man cry? I waited about twenty minutes or so and she comes out of the kitchen carrying a large tray of cakes and cookies. She was helping them prepare. She looked beautiful. Trim, slim, long black hair, very sophisticated, tall, almost my height, walked slowly in stride like a model, great face, smart looking, eyes starring and piercing, boy I was hooked. She walked over to the table I was sitting at with Walter, the entertainment secretary. She looked at me and said a big 'You?' I thought she was going to drop the tray! I reached up to catch it and grabbed her hand instead. She just looked at me. I was a very handsome young man, just so you know."

"Very modest, very unassuming."

"Performers, good actors, good artists, we know we are skilled in what we do, we are keenly sensitive to aesthetic values, but never humble, and yet never an air of bravado."

"Okay genius, continue."

"That to, Gill!"

Gill nods his head and smiles, so does March. "Anyway, she pulls away from me and turns to walk away. I get up and walk after her, not a word said. She walks into the kitchen, I push the doors open for her and she turns and smiles at me. I thought I was in heaven. 'Why are you here?' she asked with ice in her voice. I take an envelope out of my pocket and hand it to her. It's an invoice for six thousand dollars from me to the Nights of Columbus. I tell her I'm sorry for my actions and would she please accept the check attached. I never cashed the check she gave to me. She just stares at me with a fixed gaze. I didn't know if she was conspicuously telling me to fuck off again, or she was apparently glad at what I did. I just didn't know what to think. Her gaze continued for six hours, maybe ten seconds, I don't know. I was ready to accept defeat, turn and walk away. Another few seconds passed, she puts down the tray and kisses me, a real kiss. We were married three months later. Went to Europe for two weeks on our honeymoon. She moved in with me after we got married. We had a real wedding. Lots of celebrities were there everybody wanted to come but my parents. They were in their late seventies and didn't want to bother with something as trivial as my wedding. Elizabeth called them, offered to put them up at a 4 star hotel, send a limo, pay for their clothing and give them five hundred dollars for their trouble, so they came. Elizabeth met them for the first time at the wedding. I had an apartment on 75th Street and Park Avenue, in Manhattan. Elizabeth refurnished it to her liking and it was synchronized with my feelings, so all was well. We took many trips together all over the world and I started doing premium shows. Europe was great for me. Some of the audiences were over thirty thousand, we did the shows concert style. Twenty dollars average for a ticket meant we sometimes took in six hundred thousand to nine hundred thousand per show and I owned the show. Lock, stock and barrel, full of money. We were both doing things, meaningful things, we had a purpose and our intent on almost everything was of the same mind. My life was wonderful, marvelous, and amazing."

"What about the club, Lights Out? Who was running the club and the shows, what about the other clubs in the syndicate?"

"Well the sixties were here, people were watching television and going to the movies, Broadway Shows. The clubs were dying, very slowly but they were dying. It was over eight years old, Lights Out. Joe made his money back many times over. Besides the novelty of the clubs had run its course with Joe and he didn't mind if they closed. However they ran on for another few years, continuing to bring in revenue, smaller than before, but still somewhat productive. As the years went on the shows faded, turned into showcases for new talent, such as it might be."

"Who ran the shows? You were becoming a world figure. You didn't need them anymore."

"I still felt a loyalty to the clubs and to Joe Banorluga. They were almost automated by then. We changed the format every few months. Rotated the acts between the clubs. At one time there was over ten of them, ten clubs in five states; some money machine, hey Gill?"

"You worked them all?"

"Yes, but only one still open now, after fifty

years or so. It's on Flatbush Avenue. I still go there, every six months or so. Do a two hour show, just for fun. The nightclub features only headliners, big names. When I go there I work for scale, you know, union wages."

"Joe still has his office in back of the club?"

"Yes, but his office is now in Federal Prison."

"Did Elizabeth ever meet Joe?" Did she know you were working for gangsters, for the mob?"

"Oh sure, Joe would visit us often in our apartment on Par Avenue. He would bring his wife. They got along, would talk into the early morning, while Joe and I played poker. Other couples were there, too."

"Important people?"

"Senators, doctors, lawyers, Indian chiefs, lots of people. Big city contractors, broadcasters, anybody Joe could use or he could pay off was in my apartment at one time or another. Just playing cards with the mob. Nice city, nice country, nice systems. Pay offs, anything to make something you need work for you, and out in the open, so what?"

"Just like congress today!"

131

"Almost as bad." They were both having a momentary giggle, suggestive of foolishness. Two old men still not grown-up.

"So you and your wife were pals with murder incorporated. The black hand, the Cosa Nostra."

"Yes, we functioned well. When I worked in the store on Madison Avenue, my boss asked me to partner with him on a small run about boat. He knew I worked nights at the club. He also knew I had money and I could buy anything, anything I wanted. So I bought a boat. It was a small 17 ft. Thompson Lap side, almost like a rowboat. It had 2-35 H.P. synchronized, Evinrude outboards. Very fast little play toy with a canopy cover that folded down. I got used to the water, I liked it. Joe went out and we took our wives and went up the Hudson River to West Point; a nice day trip. Joe liked the water and he bought a 90 ft. yacht. He named it 'March On' in my honor. How nice, my name on a mafia boat."

"I told you so March, some day you would become a legend, a floating symbol, a pure unadulterated humble symbol of someone, maybe a criminal, maybe a killer, but a symbol! For good or bad."

"Shut up Gill, or I'll have you killed by drowning."

"Oh, oh I better listen!"

"Yes, just listen. I don't remember anything. I have a bad case of C.R.S."

"What's that March?"

"Can't remember shit."

"Anyway it's been a pleasure, a good friendship, hey March?"

"You're so right Gill, tonight you can sleep with me."

"Okay what time?"

"Hey Gill, you write the story I do the jokes." They both broke into a laughter, a giggle, their momentary giggle.

"You told me Joe Banorluga was in prison, want to tell me about it?"

"Soon, I'm leading up to it. Not there yet."

"Gill nodded his head in understanding. Tell me about Europe March, you have a house in Europe?"

"Yes I do. In Italy, on the Tuscany coast. Old stone house used to be a castle. It's a cold, windy area, but I love it. Peaceful, quiet, lovely. I go there for a few weeks almost every year."

"Just peace and quiet? Boring, what do you do there?"

"I paint, I'm a painter."

"Really March, I didn't know that. Do you sell your paintings?"

"Yes, in Europe. I'm fairly well known!"

"How come I never knew, never read about March Krantz, the artist?"

"Never told you Gill, just a little side thing I do. It's one of my hobbies, I sell under the name of Mario Lubette."

"More money. How much do they sell for?"

"Oh about fifty thousand to two hundred thousand."

"You never told me you were an artist, a celebrated artist!"

"Just in Europe Gill. I'll bring one here for you,

when I go to Italy. Probably in a few weeks."

Gill scratched his head. "I never knew, I never knew!"

"That's why the interview, right Gill?"

"What do you paint?"

"Sidewalks, giraffes, pickles, stuff like that."

"Come on March tell me. No jokes."

"Okay fine. I paint seascapes, landscapes, sometimes and people.

"Anybody I know?"

"Elizabeth and celebrities when they come to visit. Sometimes I like to drive to Vatican City to paint church people. They have great expressions, great clothing. I take pictures along the way, I follow the coast to Rome."

"What in hell do you do with all the money you make?"

"I give it away, pay taxes, and buy homes. You know I have about fifteen cars, don't you?"

"I know you have a handful, but I didn't know it was fifteen. What's your favorite?"

135

"1949 Buick convertible with white interior. I love that car."

"Where is it?"

"Here in the garage. I'll show it to you tomorrow, when the sun's out. It's too cold now."

"I don't drive it when there's snow on the ground. Don't want to damage the paint or anything on that car."

"What's it worth, March?"

A cool one hundred fifty thousand, maybe more at auction. It's a beauty."

"A cool one hundred fifty thousand?"

"Right now a cold one hundred fifty thousand, when the weather warms it'll be worth a lot more. It's a convertible."

"Another hot story, March?"

"You're becoming a comic Gill. Just hang around, it's catching."

"What was the first car you owned? Your Pontiac with the bedroom back seat?"

"No, I had a 1939 Chevy. It was a stick, my

father's car. His first but he couldn't drive it. He didn't know how. He was taking lessons from a friend of his and I would sit in the back seat and watch. I caught on very fast, but he never did. So it became my car. All I needed was my license. At sixteen I went with my English teacher to get the license the first time. I hit a car backing up to park. I asked the driving inspector if I failed after I hit the car. He looked at me with daggers in his eyes; real hatred. 'Just get the hell out of here!' He was yelling not wanting to get involved with the accident. The car I hit was parked. Then next try I got my license."

"Was that your only encounter with your '39 Chevy? Sounds like it's the car of the devil."

"Rightly so, very true to reality. You know I come from Brooklyn? We never had a car, I never rode in a car until I was seven. I knew next to nothing about the maintenance of the damn machine. So the brakes went out and I had no money to repair anything."

"So what happened? You hit somebody?"

"No, just a tree in front of the house. It was my stopping tree! I used it to stop the car."

"Really?"

"Oh yes, I took pictures of the crumpled fenders. I'll show them to you."

"You're a crazy person March. A little nuts!"

"Yes, I guess so. I'm not boring! You know that!"

"Sure do, March. Shut up and keep talking."

"How do I do that?" March was laughing out loud. Gill just smiled at him.

"We junked the car, but not before I took the motor apart to see what was inside. After I put it together there was a few springs and small parts left over. I couldn't figure out where they went, so I just threw them away."

"How did you get the Pontiac, the car with bedroom back seat?"

"I had odd jobs. Worked in the factory where my dad worked, unloaded trucks, worked for channel masters who they made T.V. antennas. Remember they called them rabbit ears? They were on roof tops all over America."

"You worked in Ellenville?

"Yes not far. All after school jobs, or after I

graduated high school."

"You graduated high school? Tell me about high school."

"Well I graduated Ellenville High, isn't that enough?"

"No March, I need material. I'm writing a story about you."

"You're right. Good luck, old man."

"Go on."

"Well high school was a task for me. Difficult, arduous work. I was incorrigible, I never knew what I was going to face, what insurmountable obstacle I would encounter that I could not deal with. I was scared, scared of my future, scared of going into the business world and not able to support myself. I was not secure in any way and I felt I had no one to fall back on."

"Any ambition, anything you were interested in doing, anything you wanted to be, to become?"

"An architect."

"Really, an architect?"

"One of my teachers talked me out of that. He

said I would go no further than a draftsman, a designer. I have a feeling now, that he was right. I also wanted to be a writer. Write funny stories or short stories for magazines."

"That didn't work, did it?"

"No it's a steel door, no one gets through it. At least in my case."

"So on to New York and a park bench?"

"That's me, except for a tiny stroke, a shot of luck from the Gods."

"The corrupt Gods, the mob Gods!"

"True, my luck."

"A great deal of misfortune for many others."

"Also true, but I had nothing to do with it. I didn't sanction anything they did."

"Not directly, but you did comply. You lived and you benefited from Joe Banorluga's actions."

"True, but I…"

"March, you're too smart a man to believe you were an outsider looking in! You said everyone in the organization talked to you. How in your mind can you claim innocent to their events? You did no wrong directly, but you were not free from sin. You were and you are morally wrong. Remember the Nazis?"

It was too much for March to deal with, he just walked out of the room, into the kitchen. He poured himself a cup of coffee but didn't drink. He covered his face with his hands and cried, cried like a newborn. Gill heard him and walked into the room after a little time passed. He put his hands around March. March looked him in the eye and smiled. It was a dry, absent look. A look of defeat.

"A cover-up never works March. I am sorry I brought it up, but it needed to come into the open. You can't keep everything in a tin box."

March turned away from Gill. "You're right, I know that. It's just such a hard fact to deal with. I never talk about my moral associations, it hurts."

"Are you sorry I spoke out?"

"No, not you old friend. It needs to come into the light. I never face anything directly and it always builds up. It hurts, but that my life."

"You did well for yourself. How many homes? How many cars?

141

How many suits? How big a bank account, what else do you want?!"

"Someone to talk to! A live warm body to sleep with. No, a hot body. Maybe a grandchild or two. Some long time, deep association."

"At your age most people are alone and struggling."

"Still I want it!"

"Did you ever consider marrying again?"

"Yes, many times. You know I married a second time after Elizabeth died? About five years later. I never got over losing her. She was the best thing any man would want."

"I was at that wedding March. The second Mrs. Krantz also. Tell me about you and Elizabeth."

"Elizabeth and I were on the same wave length for the twenty years we were married. A very good, very favorable well intentioned marriage. That was a union made in heaven. A juncture of souls."

"What happened to your bride?"

"We were in Sardinia in the village of Albia. We rented a fishing boat, captain and fishing gear

and made due north toward Corsica. The captain
said the weather was perfect, superb! He lied. I
guess he just wanted the money and didn't care
about anything else. There was another couple with
us. Friends, a doctor from New York with his wife
and teenage daughter. We were about 30 kilometers
off Corsica heading for the Liqurian sea when the
storm his us hard. The boat was a 35 ft. fiberglass
hull with an inboard diesel and not in very good
condition we were about to learn. The winds
bounced us about and the waves were splashing
over the sideboards. We were taking on water. After
ten minutes or so the ocean was winning and we
were taking on more water, the water was very cold.
The pump was starting to overheat and you could
hear the bearings grinding against each other. Then
the noise stopped. The bilge pump was dead. The
engine had stopped, it was flooded. We were almost
dead in the water. The boat was rolling as much as
60 degrees to the side. The sea flipped her on her
back, loaded with water and she sunk. Everyone
went sliding into the Mediterranean. I never saw
Elizabeth again. The teenage girl was lost also.
Everyone else was saved by rescue boats. The
captain was charged with murder by the Italian
police. He should have never taken out that boat in
that condition, in that weather."

Strange thing, Elizabeth and I had a small dog. A Pomeranian with a bushy tail, like a fox with a fur coat that was too big for its size. Anyway I came back to our place on Park Avenue and picked up the dog, Buddy, at the kennel. When he saw me, he just starred. I have picked Buddy up from the same kennel, many times. He would bark, jump, rub against my legs, stand on his back paws; all kinds of greetings. This time he just looked at me as if he knew she was gone. Strange, strange feelings. Anytime I came home after that he would jump on my lap, but no barking, no face licking, no greetings of any kind. Just the look of sorrow and grief. The poor dog was suffering as much as I was. We both were in mourning.

Chapter 19

It was the 70s, and Gessepie Banorluga, the don, laid back, not really doing anything anymore. Joe was the force behind the don, the real boss, the boss of bosses; the "Don Pedro". Gessepie could not shake off his past. His son Joe knew his father was always in danger, always being followed. His past was clinging to him like the smell of dead fish. The brine of the past, the garbage of the rotten. Gessepie had no fear, he was well into his eighties, fearless for himself but mindful of his family and their exposure to harm. His sons and his people were his concern. He remembered his brother, the brother who was pushed off the roof so many years ago over money, less money than he made in a few seconds today. Was all this necessary in his life? He wondered.

March Krantz had social encounters with the don several times in their pasts; at parties, weddings, christenings. He read a story in the papers about Gessepie shortly after Joe phoned him and told him the news. His father was in the hospital, not expected to live. He was shot in the stomach, by a guy with a shotgun in his sleeve. No one knew the man, Joe suspected it was not a mob figure because it was only one person, but who knows! Joe told him not to come to the hospital. The justice people would be watching, taking movies of anyone. So March stayed away. The F.B.I., the justice department, they all knew March had some association with the organization. They just didn't know how far it went and to what degree.

Gessepie Banorluga was near death. After 5 days in the hospital the doctors could do nothing else to save him. He called in his five sons and told them he was sorry they didn't have a better life. He said it was hard making an honest living when you're a criminal.

Then he told everyone but Joe to leave the room. Gessepie told Joe about the money he had in banks, loan companies he owned and cash he had hidden. Gessepie said he thought it might be around one hundred million or so; he wasn't sure. Joe left the room. Then Gessepie closed his eyes and never opened them again.

The media had stories about the Banorluga

146

family. It was interesting copy, people thought the Costinostra was exciting and different. Like an old West shoot-em-up.

The F.B.I still didn't connect March Krantz with the Banorluga bunch. They knew about his nightclub gigs and the shows in Europe and the states, but no connections to activities with the mob. They had no crimes committed and no evidence for direct action, so far.

The Feds telephoned March, they wanted to talk to him. They would pick him up in the car, off the street. March met with Joe and told him the feds wanted to talk.

 "Fine, okay with me. You know nothing. Talk to them, tell them whatever they want, just don't shoot off your mouth. Don't add anything, don't embellish the conversation, play it cool. Got it?" Joe said.

"Sure thing Joe. I got it." March knew how this worked.

"Keep it straight, keep it honest, okay?"

March was to meet them after his work at the

store. At six thirty, on Madison Avenue and 59th street. They pulled up to the curb with a modified limo. A Chrysler New Yorker. It had jump seat like a taxi. Not very comfortable, but it could seat eight people. March was told to get in the back, on one of the jump seats. They introduced each agent, including the driver. Then they drove around the city for almost an hour. The car had a reel to reel voice recording system, wired throughout the car. There were four agents in the car, all nicely dressed, polite, soft spoken young men. March was impressed, but still very mindful of his conversation with Joe. They asked basic questions, nothing incriminating, nothing leading, general information. The car stopped at Madison and 59th street, March shook hands all around and got out of the Chrysler; interview over.

"That's it?" Joe said "I guess you're in the clear."

"I paid up all my taxes, everything, here and overseas."

"Good boy, that will help you."

Nothing to fear from the Feds? Joe knew he was next in line. He was ready for the grilling, it had taken place many times. Not in the car, sometimes in the F.B.I offices, sometimes in the city jails. Still nothing to connect him directly with anything. Royal Sampson had covered the tracks of everyone. So far so good, they were certain all was well with Joe and the mob. Everything was covered, everybody was certain. Everybody except Joe Banorluga, his gut feeling told him Royal had let something get by him, something the Feds would catch. He didn't know why or what, but something!

The feds had asked March about details of the clubs. Their operation, their income, their payouts. It was similar to a tax audit. March wasn't told, two of the men in the car were I.R.S. tax auditors. They were looking for something, anything to incriminate Joe and his mob family. The clubs were basically an all cash business with a very high return. The mark-up was extraordinary and the expenses were monitored very carefully by Royal Samson and his staff. The high mark-up was the problem overlooked. Royal paid taxes, but on half the income from the clubs, yet they still showed a profit. They bought supplies to run the clubs. Food, tablecloths, electricians to fix the lights and change the bulbs, salaries for the hired help. Most of it but not all paid by check, almost half with cash. The feds followed the delivery trucks back to the source of supply. They noticed the clubs delivery never changed, the same amount each time, the same order. They talked to the suppliers. Actual information was given to the Feds. It was the info they needed, they wanted. The suppliers were given warning not to reveal anything to anybody. Scared to silence.

The investigation took several months of preparing, probing and further inquiry. The legalese had to be perfect. Joe Banorluga had lawyers on retainers, ready to engage and tie-up the court. The Feds knew they needed an air-tight case. Over the last sixty years or so, the Banorlugas had covered and recovered their tracks. They were experts at what they did and they did a great deal, covering all phases of their operation. There were money payouts, scare tactics and if necessary death. No concern to them, it was a business decision. Complete the mission, any method, all methods were used to gain an end. Because of the cover-ups by the Banorlugas over the years there was no action taken against them, however the Internal Revenue Service saw a different angle: taxes. They took the lead in the investigation, compiling the information needed for their case. Using the Lights

150

Out and the other key clubs as examples of money collected, money paid out, and taxes paid or not paid. The essential element was the volume of supplies and food. The IRS did their calculating based on the information gathered over several months, compiled the dollars needed to support the club's purchases and used the difference as revealing evidence in their thrust to produce an indictment which could be submitted to a grand jury by the prosecuting attorneys. At long last the IRS, in connection with the justice department, felt they were able to prosecute the Banorlugas without any criminal and or unusual problems. In other words no agents would be killed. You do not make war on the U.S. government.

Chapter 20

"The proceedings were to be conducted by two agencies with operatives from the New York Police Department, state, and federal agencies with state and federal prosecutors heading the procedure, trying to keep all information under strong lock-up. They held their meetings in cars, hotel rooms and when necessary in the federal building in Brooklyn. No two people working on the same project were allowed to enter the building at the same time."

"Super secretive, just like in the movies, hey March?"

"Only this was very serious. If any information came back to the mob they would strike back. Many people would be in danger of losing their lives, including peace officers.

The tentacles of the organization spread all over the city and in some way effected every legitimate operation in the four corner states. Every pound of butter and every loaf of bread was tied to the mob. All tied to the misery and deeds of bad faith of those people."

"It was time. Too much power for too long!"

The proof of the crimes were unveiled and shown to the public. The feeling was they must pay for their crimes."

"So March, you never were on his side, though you drank from the same cup?"

"Yes, in a way. I sat with him and his, but only on social gatherings. Yes I do take responsibility for my interactions with him and his family. Paradoxically I suffer mentally, not physically. I know if it wasn't for his kindness and good faith I would still be on that park bench. But I do not condone his actions, his life style and his non-support of the human race."

"You're a troubled soul, March."

"So I am, I guess. Everyone, to some degree, has a warped mind and a troubled soul. Life is a study of longing and of wanting. I realize now how lucky I am in the last race."

"You have many races March. Keep moving, keep racing old man."

"Thank you for your continued support, old man. I appreciate the fact that we both are still here on good mother earth."

153

"So do I March, so do I. Tell me, did you give testimony?"

"Yes I testified but there was nothing for me to affirm. In fact, at trial Joe smiled at me, and I at him, nothing said. He was convicted. There was so much evidence it was almost overbearing to sit through the trial, but I did."

"The main thrust, the key motive of the trial, was it based on taxes?"

"It was based on taxes, that's the way all this came into play, but it wasn't the way it ended. It was a big headline story for many weeks. It was front page and on the radio, television, everywhere. People from the states where he did his dirty deeds, one by one, came forward with their stories. Some with evidence they gave to authorities, some with friends involved, some with their business partners, and some with hear-say. The kettle boiled over and they came and all told their narrative. They were not afraid now that they had the support of the group, and a large group, an angry group. Now they were the mob."

"So Joe Banorluga and his associates suffered the hand of American justice. They almost paid for their crimes in full hey March? An eye for an eye."

"No not completely. They weren't tried for murder, manslaughter, or physical harm to anyone. There was no proof. As was said, the tracks were covered."

"So what did they go down for?"

"Fraudulent conveyance, misrepresentation, concealment of a material fact, tax evasion under code 720. It was a crime of the Internal Revenue. Then they got stealing, theft, the felonious appropriation of another property, felony, firearm without a license to carry, racketeering, bootlegging, conspiracy... I could go on, but that was enough to put them away for years."

"What did the court give them?"

"Maximum on every count. It added up to one hundred fifty-eight years for Joe, Royal Samson thirty years, Joe's brothers got thirteen years each and about eight to eleven years for most of the family. The happiness and exhilaration overpowered captain Manny Schwartz of the 36th precinct. His lifelong dream came true. The charges took two hours to read."

"You came away clean?"

"Yes, except for the judges reprimand and my

apologetic, remorseful repentance to the court. I was truly sorry for my years of association with those people. The trial took over four months and it taught me much more than I knew before the exposition."

"You're lucky you didn't get caught in the web. You were near the trap of deceit yet somehow you evaded it all."

"It was more than luck Gill. I was on many, many T.V. talk shows, radio interviews, newspaper conferences, town meetings, you name it. Wonderful proclaim, the publicity helped my career immensely. I had a lot of rapport to be put away without evidence. I realized everything could have worked against me but I sold two songs, big, big money.

"Do you ever speak to Joe, write him?"

"No he is in Leavenworth. He told me not to write or call him. He said, 'It is what it is, leave it alone!'"

"How old is he now?"

"A little older than us. In his late eighties or early nineties."

"A lifetime ago!"

"Not a life time for everyone. The prosecutor said to me they could have killed as many as thirty people but who will ever know?"

"All that wasted years ago or so?"

"More like fifteen. Most of the family is out on the streets again, or dead."

"God help us all March."

"Not everyone is deserving of help. They got far less than they should have gotten. They had many, many public officials in their pockets that helped somewhat with the lighter sentences. It was cover-up for a price."

"So we're through with that stage of life, hey March?"

I don't believe that at all, Gill. Just a small piece of the workings of our society. It's a big country, about three hundred million people. There will be many more exposes, both public and private."

"Explain that, will you March?"

"There are crooks operating in all types of

organizations from banks to Doctors to merchants to politicians."

"No March not politicians, oh my."

"Politicians wanting to gain power, either political or monetary. The big shame of the country is the political scene. The beneficial advantageous serve usually one person or one group. Screw everyone else."

"So you feel the human race is finished?"

"No, but we need truth in our lives. We need assumed reliable people who will help to certify our reactions, not allow the Joe Banorlugas to fester in our world."

"And how is this to happen?"

"Look up, look down, I really don't know the answer. Human nature is the overwhelming factor."

"Next subject March, one that is on a manageable level with our minds!"

Chapter 21

They took the '49 Buick, put the top down and drove into town to have lunch.

"I thought you didn't drive the car with snow on the ground and the top down in this weather?"

"I'm just showing off. If I get any dents you will pay!"

"Up yours March, put the top up, I'm freezing."

"Cold air is good for old men. You'll sleep better tonight!"

"If I don't sleep forever."

"Shut up and enjoy."

It was about three miles to the diner. Gill had trouble getting out of the car. He was frozen stiff.

"You son-of-a-bitch, you tried to kill me."

"Did it work? You seem to be still alive. When we drive back to the house I'll take the long way. That may kill you."

March held the door open for Gill Grayson.

159

There was a couple sitting at a table just a few feet away from March and Gill. The woman said to the man,

"Look who's sitting at that table!" She was pointing. "It's March Krantz, the comedian!"

"So?" Said the man.

The woman walked over to their table and gawked at March. He was used to ogling, he looked up and smiled at her. She was dumbfounded, just gawked.

"Do you want an autograph?" He asked.

She slightly nodded. He signed a napkin for her and she left, still looking back at him.

"The price of fame." said Gill.

"I love it." said March.

"Wonder of wonders. I'm sitting with a man of greatness, popularity, money and prominence."

"Okay Gill, that does it. You walk back to the house. In the morning I'll send a blood hound, a jug of whiskey and an ambulance to find you."

"You sure?"

"Maybe."

They ordered soup and coffee. The waitress knew March.

"You in town for a while March?" she asked.

"Few days, then it's off to the city. I'm filming a variety show for the holidays. Wintertime in New York. It's a two hour show. An extravaganza complete with singers, dancers, some top name people. All great acts. Want to come to see, Betty? I'll send a studio car for you."

"Thanks March, you're always great." He just smiled at Betty. Later he left her a twenty dollar tip. She kissed his cheek as they left. Back into the cold, March closed the convertible top. Gill thanked him and said he just saved the cost of his funeral. March pulled the car into the garage and turned on the space heater he had built it to meet the Connecticut winter. They sat down in the study, turned on the fireplace and had a tumbler of Haig and Haig, pinch bottle.

"This will get you going." said Gill.

Chapter 22

"So, what happened with your second wife, what's her name?"

"I need more scotch if I'm going to talk about Sue."

"How did you two meet?"

"I was invited to a dinner party. Last minute invite. I had nothing planned for the evening so I went. It was a very fancy apartment, two floors on Sutton place near the East River in New York. Number 2 Sutton Place, loaded with big name people. I had my chauffer drive me. I was apprehensive I would be able to get a cab after the dinner."

"You had a full time chauffer?"

"No, a service. I paid monthly and they always had uniformed men ready to drive you. It had to be your own car, short notice was okay. You paid for that."

"Go on."

"Need more scotch!"

"Don't get drunk and fall asleep, I need you to talk!"

"Okay boss, more coffee, okay?"

"Okay, go on."

"It was a black tie event."

"Why?"

"Don't ask me why, I don't know. Birthday, wedding, divorce, death celebration, bankrupt, new baby, who knows? I was there, one of a hundred lost souls."

"Go on."

"A lot of celebrity people. I knew most of them, said hello. There were some wonderful singers and a five piece band. They were playing one of my pieces. 'Oh so close to me, I held you tenderly. As two hearts beat as one, we were in love!' The singer was there with her husband, Steve. She had one of the best vocal cords in the business. She knew me and asked me to come up to the stage, such as it was. I was introduced to the crowd and suddenly I was not alone. People were gathering around me. I love the attention, you know."

"You're a little boy in a grown body. An old body!"

"Yes I am, and I will never divert. Take me the way I am or leave me alone!"

"Okay, okay, okay, keep going."

"There, I saw her. A pretty blonde, small build, prancing around and talking and smiling to everyone. Nice figure, slim legs. She slithers over to where I'm standing and smiles, all 32 teeth shining at me."

"Pretty, hey March?"

"More attractive than pretty. She was cute."

"You just told me nothing."

"One man's poison is another man's cheesecake, does that help you?"

"Forget it, she's pretty!"

"Okay Gill, glad you like her, I'll give you her phone number, okay?"

"Forget it March, go on, if you please."

"You're in a sullen mood, why?"

"The open convertible, I think I'm catching a cold!"

"Sorry Gill, but you know I really tried to kill you. Freezing to death is an awful way to go."

"I think it's true. Keep going."

"Well you now know her name, remember her?"

"Yes, I do. She started talking to you, broke the ice?"

"She was sizing me up. Trying to see if I fit in her scheme, in her lifestyle. I told her I traveled quite frequently and that I had a home in Italy. She liked all of that, it fit. She never asked me what I liked, it was all her. But my guard was down, I wasn't looking for anyone. I had my one night stands, that was enough for now. Everything was taken care of for me. My people cared for my three homes. The New York apartment, Connecticut and Italy. Everything was going great and life was okay."

"So blessed are we, lucky you."

"Yeah, I guess so. Anyway we talked, she dominated my time, and control was her rule.

People came over to talk and she was so talkative and loquacious, no one could stop her. An actress I did a picture with about twenty years prior tried to break into the conversation and she wouldn't let her speak a word. She was the constraint, the repressor. I told her I had to go pee and she took my arm and walked me to the men's room. I had a feeling she would hold it for me too, if I let her. I wondered if I should go home. It was early, just after ten so I said I'm going to stay, no witch is going to push me out. I still had a few people I wanted to talk to. So I puffed myself up and walked out. She was still waiting for me. Why me? I excused myself, telling her there was an old friend I must talk to. She gave me a very cruel look. I was unyielding and just walked away to the other side of the extravagant room and found someone I knew just to idly talk. Escape at last. At least I thought so."

"Trapped with a monkey on your back?"

"No I thought the monkey had left the scene and the way was clear for me to roam free. So I walked and talked with a vigilant eye, mindful of the danger."

"Sounds like a war zone March, was she that bad?"

"For me, yes. I didn't need attention, I craved company not maternal protection. Many sophisticated souls at the gathering, the essence of life for me. I stayed till one o'clock, found my driver and went home. Good evening except for madam assertive."

"But it wasn't over, was it?" Somehow you two crossed the same track again, after all you married."

"We all make mistakes."

"How did this one come to be?"

"Sue ran a bio on me."

"Smart woman, wants to know what and who she is getting involved with!"

"Shouldn't it be whom?"

"Cut it out, March, we are talking serious stuff here."

"I would have never known!"

"So she ran a biographical on you? What happened next?"

"I never would have known if one of my

associates didn't tell me she was snooping. She asked everyone in show business about me, and she knew a lot of people. It seems her ex-husband was an entertainment lawyer at one of the big firms, Century City, over one hundred attorneys. He was the executive managing partner. He owned the place, except for a few shares. Very, very wealthy. She handled everything for him and when he died she got it all."

"How did he go, cancer?"

"Heart attack."

"How do you know all this?"

"I ran a bio on her."

"Wow, you're joking! Covers the real you March!"

"Look Gill, she was spying on me, I wanted to know why. So I told my attorney to find out everything about her, is that wrong? Turnabout is fair play!"

"Why, what was going on?"

"She met me at the party, I told you the story. Sue liked me, but she didn't want any 'hanger-ons.' When I walked away from her it tweaked her to find out more about me."

"She told you all this?"

"Yes, we went together for a few months. Good friends, except she was completely controlling. We talked, she said knew she could not let go of anything. That's why she took my arm to lead me to the bathroom. She was, and probably still is, way over the top in her relations with people."

"She's afraid of losing anyone she has any relations with. Don't you think so March?"

"Yes, that's a part of it. That's why she ran a bio on me. She wanted to make sure I had my own money, and enough so I didn't need hers. Another fanatic notion. She is very, very rich. Possibly several billions yet it still doesn't allow her to relent. She's always comparing. She liked me from the second she pushed herself into my life, but she wasn't sure I was financially secure enough for her. Hence the bio, hence her holding on so tight to me."

"You're a little over the top too, March. How long have I known you, fifty years?"

March shrugs it off.

"You cover up almost everything with a nondescript remark or a joke and money is your pet subject. I guess you can't let go of the park bench, or the basement apartment, I'm correct?"

"Let's not talk about me, to me I'm a painful subject."

"Okay March, it's your story."

"You write it, I'll tell it!"

"Okay talk. How did you two get together after the Sutton Place gathering?"

"I called the couple who had invited me to the 'gathering' as you call it. I asked for Sue's telephone number. I was told she does not give out her number, so I gave them mine. I thought she might call me. I had questions for her. Several days later I got a call from her secretary. She wanted to know why I wanted to speak to Ms. Lange. I told her and I guessed it worked. A few hours later I got a phone call from God. She said she didn't want to talk over the phone, and could I meet her for lunch? I said tomorrow would be okay, she would pick me up at my office in Manhattan."

"Limo, I guess!"

"A Rolls Royce stretch limo. What an embarrassment everyone on the street starring at us. I told her to send the limo home, we'll take a taxi. She looked at me like I was crazy. We took a cab and went to the Tavern on the Green in Central Park, had a lovely lunch, and too many drinks. We took a walk and ended up at my park bench. I told her the story of my sleeping in Central Park. She said she didn't believe me, no one ever slept in a park. I told her to forget it, let it go, don't run a bio on my park bench. She just laughed.

I understood her now, somewhat. She told me she was mid-thirties but I guessed mid-forties; and I was right. At that time I was early sixties, just to give you time frames."

Gill nodded his head to affirm.

"We did become friends, but we lived on different plateaus. She could not understand my way of life and I didn't like hers, still we existed side by side. She would call me several times a day to talk about nothing, even interrupting a rehearsal for no reason. I couldn't get her to stop calling me. I wondered why I was seeing her, I had no physical attraction and I don't think she had the hots for me. She was the rope and I was the neck, so she held on."

"So why marry her?"

"She said I was her strength and that I was her brace, her support. She said she needed me. I knew I didn't need her, but she was convenient for me. She grew on me, like a vine."

"A strange hold."

"Yes. I guess so."

"You never pushed her away?"

"No. I should have, but I didn't."

"So, how did you come to marry her?"

"She asked me, I said yes."

"Why?"

"I can't answer that. I really don't know."

"You had a big wedding?"

"Very big, too big."

"Why too big?"

"It just didn't feel right to me. Second marriage, older couple but hundreds of people. I was out of place, I felt lost. She wouldn't go for an elopement type ceremony. It had to be big and bright, not quiet and subdued. She told me it would cost over two million. I said I would pay for the wedding and she would supply her mansion in Oyster Bay but she said forget it. She could easily pay, so she did. She had a magnificent home in Oyster Bay, north shore of Long Island. It's about twenty-five miles from downtown Manhattan and other homes in California, Spain, Canada, and other points around the globe. She told me all this was now mine but we had separate bank accounts, separate deed to our homes and we signed a very tight nuptial agreement. I was a trophy husband."

The big advantage to me was her law firm. Her father had bequeathed the firm to her late husband, Jack Lange. When he died she got it all. She was on the board. Not chairman, but principal stock holder, so the decision maker. Lange's heart went south after they were married, twelve years later or so. They called her the black widow, but it wasn't true. Her father died a few years after they were married and left everything to her husband. He did a wonderful job handling the lawyer end of the firm and her the business end. They had huge offices in New York, Boston, Chicago, Houston and Los Angeles.

Sue invested in large, first class office holdings and commercial property; shopping centers. She also owned private homes she lived in and rented out to movie production companies. No one really knew how much money she was worth then and I'm sure it's the same now."

"How was the law firm an advantage to you, March?"

"They owned four large jets, two six seater jets, and three DC8's her father had bought after World War II. A small air force. If they were not being used I had access to any of them, gassed-up, ready to fly, pilot and all. A treasure trove of freedom to not go through the custom hassle. The law firm made money renting out planes. Another side business for Sue."

"Did you spend any time together?"

"No, not really to be honest. We went to affairs as a couple, but we had separate lives, business and circumstances pulling us in different directions, all over the world. Most of the time we lived apart, in one of her homes or one of mine."

"Not a consortium for marriage, don't you think? Was the marriage consummated?"

"None of your damn business, Gill! God what a question." March walked out of the room. He was furious.

Gill waited five minutes and followed him. "I'm sorry." he said.

"Sorry doesn't cut it, son-of-a-bitch."

"Okay, so what do I do now?"

"You buy dinner tonight!"

"Will that cool you down?"

"No, but it will help!" They were friends for too many years to carry a grudge. Gill didn't ask any more questions, he realized he was starting to sound like an interrogator. They watched T.V. until dinner time and drove to Stanford, about twenty miles in March's Mercedes. They dined on lobster and rib eye. After the meal March ordered a very expensive bottle of wine, to go. When the check came the waiter put it down in front of March, which he gently picked up and placed in front of Gill, smiling. It was over three hundred dollars. "I'll pay for parking," he said, a devious smile.

"We square now?" asked Gill.

"No, but we will be after breakfast."

"Then dinner again, with the top down?"

175

"You got it."

"And I get the check, right?"

"You got it."

No laughs, just big smiles, everything was okay now.

Chapter 23

March's winter show went over with a bang. An excellent show said the T.V. critics. Performers and entertainers from fifty years ago as well as today's top stars. March had given many of them their first gig, and they felt indebted to him. Gratitude flowed through the show. It made it what it was. March was the producer, director, writer, and stand-up comic. He received and deserved the accolades, and he had them all. The show was his design, he was the architect. The networks were bidding. He received an offer for a twenty-seven million dollar contract for 13 weeks, but he wanted to see what else came in. Then thirty-five million with complete control came in. It was his ball game all the way, not to mention an extra 10 million for expenses. He signed the contract.

Chapter 24

March went to live in his apartment in New York. Gill went back to work on Entertainment news and his column for the daily mirror. They would continue the narrative after the T.V. show was aired, little did he know what he was in for. That much success could overwhelm an ordinary person, may drive them to drink, or to drugs. Luckily, March had the meticulous mind of a rocket scientist and a brain surgeon. Slow, calculating, accurate, but with many faults. He could not do his own taxes, he could not spell most words, and he could not remember day to day happenings. He knew his faults and how to overcome them. He hired secretary after secretary, until he found the one he wanted; then she hired a secretary. They turned into an office full of good people, mainly ex school teachers. March trusted them all, and they all admired March and his understanding of their needs. They all felt safe, secure and comfortable in his office. He moved from his old offices he held for the last thirty years to a large, elaborate, prominent suite on Broadway and Liberty, a few blocks from the World Trade Center site. March had a short temper, everyone knew that; but it lasted only a few seconds and the day was exceptional if he was not rational. The office staff said March was one-hundred seventy-five pounds of dynamite, with a short fuse.

The shows went on, success after success, quite an achievement for March. He was known to say 'my people are my success,' but his people couldn't do anything without March Krantz. He was the jester, the comic, the actor, the clown, the writer, the M/C, the consummate producer and the cement that held it all together, and he knew it. His style was low key for a man of his acclaim. Throughout his success he always remembered the park bench, and the basement apartment.

March was inspired by the entertainers, the band, and the crowds who came to see the shows. He wrote song after song and they were big hits, more money poured in. March was an informal common-place person. He enjoyed the fame, the esteem and the ordinary people who held him in great admiration, however in spite of all that he was a sincere soul. March was a quiet, a loner, a deep thinker and a philanthropic individual.

His time was rationed, no extra allotment. His office staff made all his appointments and allocations. His objection held no merit with his staff. He understood the necessary action, but hated it. No time for March Krantz. A few minutes alone? No, a show to put on. There was much work to be done; sets to construct, time allotments to be allocated, and salaries to be decided. There were people of all designs to do all that, but the final decisions were his alone. He would buy a sandwich for lunch, sneak off to his bench in the park and enjoy the great outdoors alone in Central Park. It was something done on the spur of the moment without forethought or preparation; a free man, for an hour or so anyway.

Chapter 25

March had enough, he telephoned Gill Grayson. "Meet me at the Connecticut house. You drive up."

"Why March, something wrong?"

"I need to get away, need someone to talk to."

"Okay pal, see you tomorrow."

"No tonight."

"That bad?"

"See you tonight, we'll talk."

Summer in Connecticut. The smells of the trees, the air, the peace and stillness, it all added to the calm feeling March had. He waited peacefully and quietly for Gill to arrive. It was almost two in the morning when March saw the headlights of a car. *Good.* Gill said to himself as he saw March through the window of the house. *He's still up and waiting and he looks placid. Good.*

"Hello Gill. I can't thank you enough for driving up at night on short notice."

"I came prepared, thought you might like me to stay awhile?"

"Yes, I do, thank you."

"No thanks necessary, we're still friends. Right, March?"

"Sure we are. Now let's talk."

"Okay, ready when you are."

"Thanks. I just had enough pressure. Enough control of my soul, my spirit, I couldn't take the strain anymore."

"Aren't you in charge of everything?"

"That's the problem Gill. Too much on my head. I'm the general, the captain, the sergeant and the foot soldier. It's too much."

"You need an army. Let's talk it through."

"That's why you're here man, I need help."

"When you worked for Joe Banorluga you handled everything, and it went well."

"That was forty, fifty years ago. Besides it was less work, a smaller cast that we automated and rotated the shows."

"I see, do you still want complete control? Maybe less decisions, you're the only decision maker now, that's right?

"Yes, something like that."

"Then you need a chief of staff. Someone to receive everything that goes on, a filter person. Someone who will read the mail, handle everything, soup to nuts, sit down with you on a daily basis or three times a week or whatever is necessary to complete the projects.

"The President has a chief of staff, right Gill?"

"Yes, and for the same reason you need help. The President of the United States and the President of a firm both have the same problems and tasks, just on different scales."

"Where would I look?"

"Hire someone who did the same job. A vice president of a large firm, a retired executive, a general of the military, retired of course. Anyone who held rank of a major or above."

183

"Employment agency?"

"Yes, that's a good starting point. Pay a superfluous wage and get a loyal, self-sufficient person. Someone you can enjoy working with who will get things done without driving you nuts. You're nuts now!"

"I know that, that's why I called you to help me. I need an old friend to rely on."

"I'm here to help!"

March's office people were frantic. No March for the last few days. Where was he? Dead? Heart attack, murdered, kidnapped for ransom?! Should he have a bodyguard, if he's still alive? Who would sign the bank release for the payroll, who would sign the rent checks? Who, who, who?! They called his cell phones, no answer; he turned everything off. No interactions with anything. Where oh where is March Krantz? They wanted to call the police, but didn't want the negative publicity, so they waited. Give it one more day they said.

Gill Grayson was worried that March had gone

'over the top'. He had seen friends and people he knew overwhelmed by pressure. Some from too much money, some from not enough. He understood March and he realized he was just tired, overworked and need a change. He also had comprehensive knowledge and knew he had to notify March's office, at once.

"March, I'm going to call your office and tell everyone you're okay. It must be done!"

"Please don't! I'm not ready to go back. I need a little more time, please."

"You don't have to return to New York. Stay here, I'll handle it for you, you don't have to talk to anyone. I'll do it all, you just unwind for a few more days. Okay old buddy?"

"Okay, thank you, Gill. I'm still sort of shell shocked, you understand?"

Gilled called his office the next morning. He talked to the office manager, a bright woman who understood March's condition.

"Can you handle everything for a few days without Mr. Krantz?"

"Yes, we can. There are some papers he has to

sign, and I need some cash in the office, otherwise we are okay. The next show is in the can, everything ready to go."

"Good, great, I'll have March sign whatever you send up. Hire a messenger service. How about twenty-five thousand, would that be enough to cover everything for a few days?"

"I think so Mr. Grayson!"

"Okay, done. I'll call you at end of day and let you know how he's doing. Not a break-down, just overly fatigued, I'm sure he'll be okay."

"He needs a good assistant, an associate, a collaborator!"

"We talked about it, already being handled. Call you tonight."

XXX

Chapter 26

March was dancing around his house, full of vigor now that he had Gill Grayson to talk to. "Gill, let's go for a drive. The summer doesn't last long here. I want to enjoy it."

"Okay with me, young man."

"Good, good, we'll take the convertible and drive up the coast."

"Okay with me." Gill didn't want any more conflicts in March's world. A few more days and he would be in top notch condition. They took the '49 Buick convertible up the coast, stopping at Groton, near Mystiv to eat. Then they found a place near the water. They were having a grand old time, talking nonsense, trash talk, laughing their heads off.

"Do you realize we're two old fools, crazy people?" March said.

People were looking at the two old fools, making a lot of noise.

"You two are having a lot of fun, mind if I join you?"

187

Another old fool. "Pull up a chair, love to have you." March said. "You live around here?"

"Sure do! I live in West Mystic, about ten miles down the road."

"You fishing?"

"Sort of. Right now I'm helping the Navy with a logistics problem. You know about the submarine base, here in Groton?"

Gill looked at March and March returned the look and shrugged his shoulders, they both shook their heads in awe.

"You're in the Navy?"

"Retired commander."

"Really?" said Gill. "Yet you still work with them?"

"They need me, so I'm here."

"Sorry to be nosy…" March was curious. An old guy, like him, what was he doing assisting the military? March told himself to go slow, don't chase the fool away.

"I'm March Krantz. This fellow is Grill

Grayson." March points to Gill.

"I know who you are, I watch T.V. sometimes. And I know Mr. Grayson, read his column often. It's good stuff, smart man."

"Must be another Grayson." March said laughing.

Gill asked for his name.

"My name is James Mackin. Everyone calls me Mac." They shook hands all around.

"So you're retired from the Navy, yet you still work for them. How come?"

"Well I'm needed so I'm here. Many years ago I worked with the nuclear powered super marine people, here in Groton. Helped G.E. and others with the subs. I made them work and they now work well. They're sound and fit, but like all machines do, they need servicing. Minor repairs as they do develop hiccups at times. I burp the submarines."

"You're a contractor?"

"Yes I am, paid by one of the manufacture companies that built the subs."

"General Electric?"

"No Mr. Krantz. Electric Boat Division of General Dynamics."

"Oh, almost got it right."

"Yes, sir, you almost did."

"How is your contracting business going? You're what they call a subcontractor?"

"Very funny March. You should be on television." said Gill.

"That's an old one for me." said Mac.

"Sorry." said March. "Sometimes it just slips out, I can't help it."

"That's why you're such a well-known." said Mac.

"Well known bullshit artist." said Gill.

"You're walking home." said March.

"Again?"

"You two guys are great together." said Mac. "What a show," laughing loudly.

"Back to the subs." said Gill. "Tell us more, sounds interesting. Want a beer?"

Mac filled them in. He did work as needed, he was a specialist with the control panel, it governs the trim tanks and allows the subs to dive, surface and stay buoyant. Unfortunately the work wasn't steady. The Navy had their own crews and in most cases could take care of problems as necessary to maintain the fleet. He had his commander's pension, but was tired of fishing or doing nothing. He missed the navy's activity. He missed the performance, the accomplishments, and the conflicts. He felt his way of life was taken from him and he missed the excitement.

"You live alone, don't you?" asked March.

"Yes I do, and I like it. Even though my life is empty. I never married. My sister, Louise, lives here about three miles away. Only family I got left. We get along, she's a great gal. Mid-sixties, looks great too. I guess I'm talking too much, you gentlemen have to run along, don't you?"

"No." said March. "Keep going, you're an interesting fellow. I'm enjoying this."

"Well thank you, Mr. Krantz."

"Please call me March." They shook hands again. They appeared to have found a companion in each other. Gill was thrilled to see the two of them

191

as compatible as they were. He excused himself, went to the restroom and then took a long walk so Mac and March could talk. He came back to the table after thirty minutes and was glad to see they were still at it, talking.

"Hi Gill, where were you. Took a ride on a submarine?"

"Just walking. Novel place this Groton. Found a motel, very close, looks clean. Want to stay over?"

"Sure, nothing to do. I'm not going back to the zoo until next week, no matter what happens. Life will go on without me."

Chapter 27

They rented a suite at the motel. Kitchenette, two bedrooms and two bathrooms; money was never a concern for either of them. They would stay the weekend, or another few days anyway. James Mackin had dinner with them, the main reason they stayed over.

"I really enjoy your time here." said Mac. "Too bad you're leaving, back to New York."

"The truth of the matter, is that we want you to join us in New York. You would be perfect as second in command. What do you say?"

"I'm in shock. I didn't expect this. Let me think!"

"Take all the time you need, we will be here for another few days. We can talk further when you are ready."

"I'm in shock, what will I do in New York besides the work? What is the work? You want to build a fleet of nuclear submarines and attack Washington?"

March and Gill were both laughing, loud and

long.

"You'll do just fine. Think it over, if you want to take the job, we're here for a few days. Let us know and we will fill in the details."

"Do you two work together?"

"No, Gill and I are good friends. Known each other for many, many years. Just good friends on a short holiday."

"Why don't you two come over to my place, tomorrow night? I'll ask Louise to cook dinner, she's the best there is."

"Sounds good." said March.

"Okay Gill?"

"See you tomorrow night." said Gill.

"Something to chew on while you are pondering. The job would pay over one-hundred fifty thousand dollars plus all expenses paid."

The next day they walked around the Groton Area, again. March wrote out the duties Mac would have if he took the position. The artistic side was covered, Mac would handle the business side. Some travel was needed.

Night was slow coming, March wanted to meet Mac's sister. At long last, sunset, the sun splashed into the ocean, not a sound was heard.

March and Gill followed the direction given to Mac's house; a country home, very warm look, wood all over, almost a log cabin, made of concrete and oak. March felt very good, a feeling brought on by the prospect of Mac working for March's organization, true relief.

The house smelled wonderful, cooked apples and homemade bread and other things, cooking.

"Come in, come in you two, meet Louise."

A smiling, good looking woman. Trim and full of life and vigor. March was overwhelmed for a few seconds. The smell of the home, the greeting, the look of the house, clean, neat, what an extraordinary evening this was promising to be.

Louise was surprised when she first saw March. He looked nothing like the man she had seen on T.V. He was taller, slimmer and more

195

sophisticated in person. She was startled, she expected among every other wrong impression, an older man. March, though close to eighty, looked like he was in his late fifties, early sixties. Good living, good health so far, and good doctors all helped, along with the millions he had to support his lifestyle.

Louise baked a breast of veal, stuffed with a bread and potato filling.

"Are you getting hungry?"

The oven smells, along with everything cooking could drive you to kill. It was wonderful.

Louise served, Mac helped, and March and Gill joined in. Truly a family affair. They ate for an hour, talking and joking. Mac told war stories and Louise was nodding her head, she had heard them all before.

"Okay, let's get down to business!" Commander James Mackin said in his official tone.

"Sure, good idea. What do you want to know?" Asked March.

"Why me, and why one-hundred fifty thousand dollars? What's up?"

"Okay Mac, Commander James Mackin. As you probably know I put on a T.V. show. Its numbers, audience rating is very, very high."

"Outstanding!" Joined in Gill. "I want to interject, may I March?"

"Of course, as long as it has reference to the subject at hand."

"Of course March, let me continue. The show isn't just successful, it's the biggest money maker ever in T.V. land and it brings in a fortune with every show. More money for the network means more money for March Krantz. Money paid by sponsors. The more people watch, the greater sales of that company's products. March has a few hit albums and singles, how many March?"

"About ten or so top labels, about ten more secondary labels, and about ten or so other labels that still bring in revenue."

"So you see Mac, this is a very big enterprise and it's over one's head."

"I did just fine until the T.V. show caught on. It's too many irons in the fire. I need help with the financial end, the business end and someone to lighten my work load. You can't train for this job.

You have to have the basic qualities of management. This includes being able to intercede and the ability to follow through; and of course the ability to grasp the significant factors as they arise. Basic intelligence, others need not apply."

Louse was looking at March with reverence, what a smart man. March caught her look and smiled at her, then winked. She almost dropped the apple pie. March caught that too and he was staring at her now, in delight.

"So the job is really a trial run?" said Mac.

"Yes, a contract with a ninety day trial run, same salary. It has to be that way. If it works after ninety days it will pay a performance bonus and we'll sign a complete contract. Okay?"

Mac didn't know what to say. Yes meant he would move to New York City. Change his life style, give up his home and his connections with the Navy. No meant letting a wonderful potential opportunity slip by. Louise was listening and very angry at Mac. Finally she spoke, and spoke she did.

"You're a fool commander. You're afraid of something you have been doing all your life: Leading men into battle, onto situations, into conditions that you along had to deal with. Damn it big brother, go into the world! Take six months off from everything and try it, you might like it. New York was always where you prevailed. Do it again, do it!"

Mac was scared to let go of his lifestyle, everyone in the room knew it. He didn't speak. Five minutes went by. Louise served coffee and her homemade apple pie with vanilla ice cream. It worked. Mac jumped to his feet.

"Damn it, you're right!"

"Everyone was smiling. "See you in the Big Apple, Mac."

Chapter 28

The firm, March Productions, rented a two bedroom apartment in an extended term hotel, for Mac. They took a three month's lease in Mac's name, and the firm paid for it. They also leased a Cadillac Escalade. They went so far as to take the commander to Brooks Brothers and told him to pick out all the clothes he wanted. March was on Mac's side, he was really hoping it would work out. March supported everything Mac needed to make it work, and Mac knew that. The money wasn't the only thing March provided. He took Mac out into the entertainment world, introduced him to the top people who ran the business; and who signed the big checks. He made it easy for Mac to get his feet wet. Mac wasn't a follower, he was a leader. Soon, very soon he was making deals that brought in millions to March's company. He sold the show overseas to network television. He hired people and bands to perform March's songs. He put on shows with top name celebrity performers who were notable worldwide. Mac paid them a royalty and a large gate percentage as well as a base salary and lodging. He paid out a great deal of money and got a great deal in return. Mac took direction from March: Don't sit on money, make it work, increase, and spread it around.

After six months March had a meeting with his company Board of Directors. Some very influential people in banking, finance and internet. They all agreed with March and voted a million dollar bonus for Mac. March Productions was well over the billion dollar mark on its way toward several billions in assets. All in two years and all due to Mac. He was a fountain of ideas, and after approval from March, he carried out the necessary functions to make it all work. As a small incidental thought, they bought the building the company offices were in. They overpaid, knew it, and knew once they bought it the value would increase; which it did.

Mac opened offices in Beverly Hills. He set up an office in Paris and Berlin. They had enough cash flow to buy a movie studio and start making their own movies. March spent two full days talking to Mac and meeting with the board. Everyone voted it down. Too risky, they said. The business they were in makes money without risk. "Stay the course." March said.

March and Mac were having lunch at Tavern

201

on the Green. Gill would join them for desert. The conversation drifted toward Louise. March told Mac he was dating Louise. Mac knew it and was happy for them.

"And if we moved to Italy, how would you take that?"

"Not too well March. I do want to see my sister, and you. Italy is far, far away."

"I knew that Mac, I knew the answer before I asked you, but Louise and I talked it over and we're both for it."

"Why? Why Italy?"

"I love the look, the quiet life style, the country feel. I lived in a small town as a boy, Ellenville in New York State. I want to get back to that feel, but not the problems I had then, which you can read about in Gill's book."

"I read some of the transcript, Gill loaned it to me."

"Oh, so you know all about March Krantz?"

"I know what's in the book, but I don't think anyone knows all about March Krantz. So, what about Italy?"

"I have a Villa on the West Coast. I bought it about thirty years ago. It's attached to one-hundred fifty acres of land. We grow olive trees, vegetables, some grapes, and we make a little wine for our own consumption. It's mountainous, not farm land, but it keeps everyone busy. We have four families living on the land, they take care of everything and keep what they sell. I also give them a few Euro to live on. I built houses for them and they raise goats, chickens and sheep. For me it's ideal living until the end of my life."

"You going there to die? Something wrong with your health?"

"No, I check out just fine. I'm healthy, wealthy and stupid.

Life is good, and with you running everything, everything is just ducky, thank you."

"You're Villa is near Piombino?"

"I've been there in a submarine, through binoculars, but also in Florence. I toured the museum and art on leave as a tourist."

"You and Louise are two very lucky people."

"Then you approve?"

"I really can't say no. Two adults, and she is not my daughter, she's my sister. Will you get married?"

"No, no reason to. At our ages and with March Productions, it would get very complicated."

"I guess I can fly there, you have rooms to put me up if I come for a few days?"

"More rooms than you can count. It's a castle three stories high, with towers that I'm converting to guest rooms. You will love it."

They hugged just as Gill walked over to their table.

"So there you are." said March. "We were wondering what kept you."

"Look outside, there's paparazzi all over the place! They followed me to get to you."

"Everyone has to make a living. I'll talk to them on the way out."

"You're too nice March."

"Someone has to be nice around here."

"More jokes, you too guys are so silly, I love

it." Said Mac.

"Let's go." Said March.

"Where we going?" Said Gill.

"The office. You've never seen the new offices, have you?"

They took a cab downtown. The building was very clean, March was a clean freak. Once every three months the building was steam cleaned. Many national figures, executives, and top show people went to March Productions for business meetings. They talked to people about shows pending and sponsors about money and contracts. Star power was the order of the building and March Production. The building has glass all over the lobby. It was very bright and sunny on sunny days; marble, a typical New York successful look. Mac built a large fountain in the lobby and there was a four foot model of a Seawolf Class submarine floating with a flag. It said, "We cover the world to bring you entertainment."

Gill said to March, "You crazy son of a bitch, why this?!" He was pointing to the fountain.

"Mac did it, he didn't tell me. I was in Norway, doing a show."

He pointed at Mac, smiling.

"Looks good…" Said Gill. "…but a little crazy."

"I caught March's sickness." said Mac.

March shook his head laughing.

They went upstairs, to the 11th floor penthouse, the elevator stopped in front of a marble, enclosed hallway. This led to March's office, and Vivian's office. Vivian was the controller and office manager for March Productions. March knocked on the door and went in.

"Hello, Vivian." She looked up at March, stood and gave March a big smile. She then walked over to him and hugged him.

"Vivian was bookkeeper, office manager, everything when we were just a small multi-million dollar company. They both shook their heads, they were now capitalized at over twenty-five billion.

"Hi boss!" Vivian said to Mac. Mac waved at her. "Come on, I'll show you the big boy toys." They walked into March's complex. Two very large rooms, one an office, one a large sitting room with walk-in closets in both rooms. March had a large, fancy bathroom, similar to one in a very expansive mansion. He was in his office just a few times a year. Most of the work was handled by Mac and his staff, exactly the way March had hoped it would work; without him. They went into Mac's office, one very large room with a large lavatory area. March sat down and hand gestured to both of them, they sat down.

"Gill, you know how old I am?"

"So what?"

"So, I'm quitting and moving to Italy. I really don't run this business anymore, it runs by the board, by Mac here, and by people like Vivian. I'm surplus, extra residue, I've out-lived my time and I know it. I don't care to hang on any longer, it can go on now without me. So goodbye everyone, on to retire in Italy."

"Wait till the street hears about this, the stock will fall to zero." said Gill.

"Wrong." said Mac. "It's a closed corporation, there are no public shares so everything is in house; March's house."

"Wow, I never knew that." said Gill.

"Just had to ask me. When Mac came aboard he generated so much cash that we bought back all our public shares."

"Wow and wow again. You guys are the shrewdest in the box. The money box, you live in."

"Commander Mack in all his doing, he is the brains. I only collect, he provides. Call in Vivian, she should hear this too." Mac pressed the phone and called in Vivian.

"What's up Gentlemen?"

March filled her in. She was surprised, she knew this would come, she just didn't know when. The commander was doing a wonderful job. March allowed him all the latitude needed to perform and perform he did. March didn't have a timeline to leave for Italy, but soon. Louise knew everything, they had a sit-down a few weeks ago and came to the conclusion they had to get completely away from March Productions. The time had come. March told the three of them he would allow one billion to be distributed to key people as bonus to be paid in June, one month away.

"Just make me a list of recommendations, in about a week. In one week, on Tuesday, we will call a press conference. Fill in the world about March

Productions.

"Why on Tuesday?" asked Mac.

"So my friend here…" March pointed to Gill. "…can get the scoop. I owe it to him."

"Thank you Buddy."

"You're very welcome Gill. I remember your coming up to Connecticut when I needed you. Just a little thank you, is in order."

"So many years ago and you never forgot?"

"How could I forget? I almost blew my fuse and you were there to hold my hand."

"Let's go on March, ancient history."

"Yes you're right." The others were looking at them both, wondering.

"No explanation, it's a long time ago."

"So when would you leave, any date set?"

"No, not yet, there are workmen in the Villa and much has to be done. I want Louise to feel comfortable. The rooms are old, cold, and raw looking. It's a very old building. A few weeks maybe, I'll let everyone know. I'm not sneaking out, just retiring."

209

"We'll make a big party, put the show on T.V." said Mac.

"What a brain, no wonder you're so successful March." Gill said. "Holy smoke Mac, want a job?"

"You can't afford me Gill."

"Neither can I." said March. "Dinner anyone? I'm buying. Louise will be meeting us at seven at Longchamp's okay?"

The four of them took a taxi to Madison Avenue. It was a little early so they walked to Lexington to kill time at Bloomingdales. March headed for the kitchen area, he was sizing up all the items Louise would want for the Villa. They would buy anything they thought they could use. Made in America and shipped by plane to Florence and then by truck to Piombino. He called his contractor in Italy to see if he could widen the road to the Villa, it was just a dirt trail and needed work. The climate was similar to the Carolinas, mid-seventy in July, mid-forties in January. Better than Connecticut or New York most of the time, who really knows. March felt it would work well for them both. He would not have to conform to the lifestyle he hated; the business world. He could enjoy the peace and quiet he craved. Louise was happy and looked forward to Italy, and they would live in harmony. She said she felt much joy in the lifestyle they were about to pursue.

March took the big plunge, he sold his Connecticut house, and Louise sold hers. He still had his apartment in New York to be used on return visits. He sold his car collection at auction. His house and his cars brought in fabulous amounts, due to the publicity of his name. March had instructed the building maintenance to remove the submarine from the fountain and replace it with a sailing ship. A clipper ship like the Cutty Sark.

"Put the flag back on the clipper ship." March took the four foot model submarine with him to Italy. It would be in the pond near the Villa another joke by March Productions, this time the joke was on Mac.

They were packed and ready to fly. They flew on his ex-wife's jet, no charge, as she promised him years before. Off they go, next stop Florence. The Villa awaits.

Chapter 29

March was working on a hillside, digging for vegetables he and Louise had planted as experimental. They had both taken to the soil, planting and growing hybrids, anything that could grow in their acreage was planted and cross-bred. They had become the ultimate farmers. The family living on the land with March and Louise thought God had sent them. They were the custodians of the land and of its people. They took care of everyone and everything. If anyone was sick a doctor would appear on the scene. New roads were built in the area. A new fire truck suddenly came to live on the property, with men to train 'March's Group' as they were often called. People all over Northern Italy had heard of the Americans and how they took care of life and limb of their flock.

March and Louise often drove to Florence, an all-day drive to stay at a hotel, eat at fine restaurants and see a play, an opera or a concert. Some days they flew to Rome to do the holiday trip. Life was good even though they both had slowed, age was catching up.

At close to ninety now March was still working

in the fields, as a farmer with his hybrid vegetables. He also was painting and selling his painting through an agent in Europe. He gave the money earned to charities, March was always a big hearted philanthropist. He said it was easy when you're worth billions. He still thought about his fortune, what to do with the money, who it leave it to? Such a problem!

March went to a local doctor every four months. It was at Louise's insistence, she knew his age and was concerned. No reason, just his age.

March again was in the field, this time with a pickaxe, digging up potatoes he and Louise had planted. Louise was digging with a shovel not far from March. He started to sweat, got lightheaded and fell down. Louise rushed to his side. He was just lying on his back, his eyes open, trying to smile, but he couldn't move. The doctor came within ten minutes; he had left another patient to rush to March.

"Looks like a stroke, I don't know to what degree. I called an ambulance."

There were almost fifty people in the lobby of the hospital, no one was allowed to see him, including Louise.

It was a stroke, the rupture of an artery leading to the brain, or a cerebral hemorrhage. At this early point they didn't know. Everyone was told to go home, they would be able to call the hospital the next day for updates. Louise stayed in the waiting room all night.

After three days there was no change. March just lied there, not moving, not talking. He looked as if he was smiling, who knows if he was clinically dead or alive. The doctors put him on oxygen tubes all over the place. After three more days they sent him home with an oxygen set up. Louise had power of attorney and wanted him home; so he could be near her. He passed away the next day.

The funeral was held in Italy; in a cemetery near March Krantz' home. The newspapers reported, without counting, that there were over one thousand in attendance. It was an international story, much acclaim was due to March and his philanthropic ways;

A true humanitarian. His shows had performers all over the world he had discovered and

Supported, talent both old and new all his career.

Gill Grayson flew to Italy and gave an Impromptu oration at the gravesite. He told of his long friendship with March and the frolic and banter between them over the years.

Not only a good man, but a true observer of the human condition, the good of men.

Many of the town's people came forward to applaud the goodness of March Krantz, the doctors support for everyone, the health clinic. The roads he had built, the fully equipped fire station and the free or very low cost housing provided to all who lived and worked on his land; the land he loved.

Louise was sad of course but also grateful that she had so many good years with March. She knew his time would come, he was at the age where every second was a blessing for him. Louise would stay in Italy on the land and continue her work with hybrid vegetables. Her brother, Mac stayed two weeks with her after March was interment. All the board members from March's company were at the funeral along with many celebrities and world dignitaries. Over two hundred people from March Krantz Productions and shows were in attendance. A man of purpose put to rest.

The End

ABOUT THE AUTHOR

Ed Halpern was born in Brooklyn, New York during the 1930's. He has written four novels, as well as lyrics, TV scripts, and poems. Ed and his wife of over fifty years live in Los Angeles, California. They have two children together and three grandchildren.

www.ingramcontent.com/pod-product-compliance
Lightning Source LLC
Chambersburg PA
CBHW060805120626
46557CB00001B/90